MAGIC PASSAGE

CHARMED

JODY SWANNELL

For my husband, Curtis.

CONTENTS

THE FOOL

"*D*ammit — I thought I could make it." I shook my head, embarrassed.

"I thought you could, too," Louis said as he opened the passenger door of my beat-up mini-van and got out to inspect the damage.

This year's snowfall was overwhelming, and my front passenger tire sank in the snow. Louis told me to turn left, then changed his mind. When he directed me to go back, I tried to pull a U-turn and ended up in the ditch.

His little sister called when we were on our way to a restaurant. She'd fought with her boyfriend and desperately needed a ride.

I felt foolish. *That's great — some first date, this is.* Louis and I worked together at the Sandberg Inn, a privately owned hotel and were friends for around a year. I suspected he had a crush on me, and two days ago, he finally got the nerve to ask me out.

He strained to push while I reversed the gear and revved the engine. It didn't budge. I knew it wouldn't; he didn't weigh much more than I did.

Closing my eyes, I conjured power from the ether to

summon assistance. I focused on the image of a car that would effortlessly come to our aid.

The High Priestess from my coven taught me that spells, props, and charms helped with magic but were unnecessary. Evidently, she was right. A set of headlights turned onto the street and parked opposite us.

Three men dressed in black with rimmed hats got out of a dark sedan and walked toward my van. I recognized them as Mennonites as they positioned themselves to help Louis push while I backed out onto the street.

I expressed gratitude to the universal energies and the men they guided. "Thank you," I called out the window.

One of the men nodded at me, and they got back in their car and drove away.

"Wow, that was lucky," Louis said, getting back into the van.

"No doubt." I smiled.

I wasn't about to tell him about the magical influence. He seemed like a realist, but I didn't know for sure. I kept my talents a secret as per Sacred Twilight's laws. Unlike my previous coven — Golden Crescent — who was pretty open about witchcraft.

After graduating from the Hotel Management course at college, I received a job offer to manage the lovely, privately owned hotel in Sandberg. This small city was almost two hours from the town where I'd lived my whole life.

Before I managed to unpack, Holly, the High Priestess of Sacred Twilight, contacted me. She enthusiastically invited me to join her local coven.

I'd already been granted the rank of the third degree in Golden Crescent, so Holly fast-tracked me through the first three degrees in Sacred Twilight. My previous experience studying magic deemed me worthy in her eyes.

I demonstrated my magical abilities for evaluation by the

High Priestess before undergoing the rituals from their unique ceremonies.

Before Holly approached me, I'd considered starting a coven. She convinced me that my level of mystical understanding was good, but I had more to learn.

She felt people's increased interest in the craft meant this city would benefit from a second coven and expressed a desire to divide Sacred Twilight. She wanted to make room for new initiates and allow her members to continue their vocation in a satellite coven with similar rituals.

"Turn right here," Louis said, interrupting my wandering thoughts.

"Are you sure?" I smirked at him.

He laughed. "Yes, I recognize this street. I don't know why I told you to turn down that road earlier. These streets all look the same, especially in the evening when it's dark."

"Excuses, excuses. That must be it — it's the only apartment building on the street," I said.

"There she is." Louis pointed.

Katie was standing outside, hugging herself tightly. There was a dusting of snow on her fuchsia pink coat and her pixie-cut hair, which meant she'd been waiting outside in the cold for some time. She saw us, skipped to the van, and jumped in the back.

"Let's get out of here," Katie said.

"You mean — *thank you*," Louis scolded.

"Right. Thank you, Sophia, for coming to my rescue." Katie wiped the snow off her jacket and buckled her seat belt. "Believe me — I'm *so* done with that loser — it won't happen again."

"I should hope not; we gave up our reservation at The Mill Steakhouse to come to get you," Louis said.

"Sorry, guys," she said.

"That's all right. We can grab something at the theatre," I said.

Katie was eighteen years old, and while I navigated through town to drop her off, Louis lectured his younger sister. She didn't seem to care what he said and called one of her friends to complain about the argument until we dropped her off at Louis's townhouse.

He moved to Sandberg a short time before I did, with the hotel offering him the position of lead Chef during its grand opening. He'd come from the small village, Henmount, just on the city's outskirts.

Katie often stayed with him to avoid the boredom of *living in the bushes with their parents*, as she put it.

Between the three of us, it was hard to decide who the *fool* was. My final trial to progress to the highest degree in Sacred Twilight was a unique Celtic spread that Holly designed. An entity she summoned to manifest itself in the physical world would influence my life until all ten cards were laid out.

She indicated it could take two to three days to complete the process. Evoking spirits was something I was eager to learn. My previous coven shied away from summoning wandering spirits or entities to manifest in the physical world, deeming it too dangerous.

Holly evoked an ancient spirit to prepare what she called a *Magic Passage*. The spiritual entity would use the meaning of the tarot cards to decide how to influence the physical world around me. When she drew a card, she would send me a picture of it, triggering an event that would actuate the next spiritual lesson.

After this trial and graduating from Sacred Twilight's fourth and final degree, I could start practising evocation. Only very experienced witches could successfully perform it. Most attempts would be met with silence; spiritual entities often ignored creatures outside their realm.

There was a danger that parasitic entities might wreak havoc on an inexperienced or overzealous witch. The first card Holly pulled this morning was *The Fool*. This could represent me or anyone close to me. I turned my head to look at Louis briefly and thought it could easily be him.

I pulled into Louis's driveway to drop off Katie. "There you go."

"Thanks, guys. Have a great time at the movies," she called out while running into the townhouse.

"What a pest." Louis rolled his eyes. "I haven't seen your friend Holly around lately. Usually, she stops at the hotel with coffee for you. How's she doing?" Louis asked.

"She's good; I was at her house yesterday. Why? Do you miss her? Or shall I say miss *seeing* her?" I laughed.

Louis didn't know Holly personally, but everyone at the hotel knew who she was. Holly was stunning. Well endowed and only five-foot-three inches, she had long dark brown hair, alluring amber eyes, and abnormally full eyelashes.

When she walked into a room – everyone stopped and stared. I doubted it was a spell, either. She loved wearing low-cut blouses to see where people's eyes focused.

"Come on, Sophia, you know me better than that," he said.

"Do I, though?" I faked pouting. "I see the guys at the hotel falling all over themselves at work to catch sight of her — some of the girls too."

"She's not my type," Louis said.

"Whatever." I rolled my eyes and laughed. "She's everyone's type."

We arrived at the theatre to find the parking lot jam-packed. We were early, and the film before our show was still playing.

I found a space at the back of the parking lot. Once inside, we shed some winter clothing and lined up to grab hotdogs, fries, and nachos.

"Not exactly what I had in mind for a first date. I'm so sorry," Louis said.

"Don't mention it. I'm used to *great* first dates; the change is refreshing."

I could see that my sarcasm didn't have its usual effect because Louis's face dropped. He used his index finger to push his glasses up after they slid down the bridge of his nose and looked at me with a sad expression.

"Oh, don't give me that look. Anyways, now you have an excuse to ask me out on a second date. This one barely counts." I winked at him.

He smiled. "*And* we'll take a cab next time we go somewhere."

We chatted about work, and I listened to him complain about his sister staying with him too often. We gathered and discarded our garbage as people started emptying the theatre.

"Looks like we can go in now," he said, finishing the last fry.

Louis chose a superhero movie that was action-packed with fantastic special effects – his favourite. I liked his geekiness and was fond of both *Marvel* and *DC* movies.

My last boyfriend, Chad, was the opposite. All he wanted to do was go to the gym and watch sports.

Louis grabbed some popcorn and soda before we seated ourselves.

"You'll have to carry me to the van after I eat this bucket." I held the massive bucket of popcorn up in the air.

He lifted an eyebrow. "Well, I thought you'd share with me, but go ahead and pig out."

I threw a greasy kernel at him, and he pretended to be offended. During the movie, I kept thinking about Holly's instructions on evocation.

Energy *obeys*. The trick is understanding that all life forms constantly express their ideas and desires—a big, tangled web of intentions worldwide. The quantum world didn't care who or what commanded it.

Knowledge *of* power *is* power, she would say. To create

something from nothing was conjuring. Enticing a living creature from the upper or lower realms to do your bidding was complicated and dangerous. Many witches succumbed to the spirits they mistakenly thought were under their control.

Lost in thought and staring blankly at the screen before me, I wasn't prepared when Louis leaned in to kiss me. I turned my head sharply because he caught me off guard, and we bonked our front teeth.

"Owe, crap, that hurt," I said, holding my mouth.

Louis abruptly backed away. "Ugh, sorry."

I started to laugh uncontrollably, and Louis just stared at me, smirking the way someone does when they see you laugh but don't get the joke. A guy a few rows back hushed me, and I settled down, wiping the tears from my eyes.

I kissed his cheek. "That was my fault; I didn't see you coming."

He put his arm back around me, and we watched the rest of the movie. After it was over, I needed to use the washroom before the drive home.

"I'll be right back," I said.

I waited in line, and after using the facilities, I turned on the tap to wash my hands. I had a sudden paranormal feeling of impending danger. *Dammit* — I thought. I wasn't trying to use the water to divine the future; it just happened. Since Holly prohibited magical instruments, the skill came randomly.

Inadvertently, I'd used the water out of habit to sense my environment. I turned the water off and looked at my reflection in the mirror. Again, I felt electrical prickling throughout my body, warning me of danger. Shaking it off, I left the washroom to join Louis, making a mental note to drive slowly on the icy roads.

We walked together, holding hands, and when I slipped, he saved me from wiping out on the fluffy snow-covered ice. "Close one," he said.

"I'm a klutz, I know."

I heard my phone chime an angel melody. It was Holly alerting me that she'd pulled the next tarot card. If she wanted to talk, she would've called. During the Magic Passage ritual, she will text me a picture of the tarot card to help me prepare for the next challenge.

I pointed my fob to unlock the van when suddenly, two dark figures popped out from behind it wearing balaclavas.

One of them punched Louis in the face hard enough that he went down immediately. I was so shocked that I didn't react at first. I just stood there for a second, watching Louis struggle to get on his feet.

I noticed a shimmer of light close to my head and readjusted my focus. I could see the street light glimmering off a knife pointing at me a few inches from my throat.

"Gimme your purse," the thug growled.

I dropped my purse in the snow, threw my hands in the air, and stepped backwards. The other guy lifted his foot and stomped Louis back down when he attempted to get up.

The one with the knife watched his partner assault Louis, and I took the opportunity to focus my energy on calling forth magic power. Clenching my fists, I imagined balls of electricity gathering in my hands — I started to rise.

"That was a great movie," a girl giggled behind us.

"Not bad," said another.

As their voices approached, the mugger lowered the knife, turned swiftly, and darted into the darkness with the other goon on his heels.

"Are you okay?" I kneeled to discover Louis had a bloody nose.

I picked up his glasses from the snow and handed them to him.

"Those bastards," he snapped. "Yeah, I'm okay. I can't believe the guy caught me off guard like that. I should have dodged his punch. Did they get your purse?"

I looked down at the purple bag in the snow. "No, the scumbags left it behind."

I suspected that my magic must have spooked them because there was no way a couple of girls scared armed robbers. I pulled out my phone to call the police. The tarot that Holly sent was on my display banner. It was the *Seven of Swords*.

SEVEN OF SWORDS

I dialled nine-one-one and explained to the operator what had happened. We got into the van to warm up while waiting for the police to arrive. I inspected Louis's nose now that it had stopped bleeding.

"Oh, I hope it's not broken."

"I'm fine — how are you? You must have been so scared. I wish I were a better fighter," he said, rubbing his head.

"I'm all right — a little shaken up." I shrugged.

Truthfully I was pissed. I'd never felt so vulnerable. Usually, I'd be wearing an amulet imbued with a hefty defence spell. My mother had given me an antique family heirloom, a beautiful silver triple-moon necklace.

Mom wore it regularly until it was time to refresh the protection spell. Unfortunately, it was sitting in a black obsidian box that Holly had provided me with. I was forbidden from wearing any amulets during the Magic Passage.

"There's the police." Louis jutted his chin toward the flashing blue and red lights in the distance.

Three police cars showed up, but the masked men were long gone. We gave our statements to a detective, who handed us his card. "You folks, take care. Please get in touch with me if you think of anything you might have missed," he said.

"Thank you," Louis said, taking the card from him.

Pulling out of the parking lot, we saw a few onlookers getting interviewed, but no one seemed to have witnessed the incident. I felt terrible for Louis; it looked like he would end up with a couple of black eyes.

"Do you want to stay at my place tonight? I'm not suggesting anything weird — I have a spare room. I just thought maybe you don't want to be alone," Louis said, clearing his throat.

"I'm okay, thank you. They didn't get my purse. I would've been nervous if those goons had my driver's license with the address on it."

"I'm shocked they didn't grab it." Louis shook his head in disbelief. "If their motivation was to rob us, why leave the merchandise?"

I scoffed. "I'd hardly call it *merchandise*. I might have had twenty bucks in there — if that. Who carries cash anymore? The second call I would've made after the cops would have been to the bank to cancel my cards. Those creeps must be desperate."

"Maybe they wanted your phone — plenty of personal information in there," Louis said thoughtfully.

"My phone *is* worth more than my purse."

When we arrived at Louis's place, I pulled into the driveway and parked to get another look at his face.

"Oh, boy, you must be sore. You're going to have a heck of a time sleeping tonight. Take some ibuprofen."

He smiled. "I'll be fine. At least he didn't knock my teeth out."

"Thank goodness. Dating a *toothless wonder* isn't out of the question, but I'd miss that smile."

"*Sophia, the Sarcastic*," Louis said. "That's your superhero name."

"Wow, that name sucks. I was hoping for a cool name after

watching a movie with mutants teleporting and shooting laser beams out of their eyes."

Louis smiled, but his face changed, and he looked serious. "I'd be devastated if those guys hurt you. I'm glad you're okay." He reached over, put his hand behind my neck to direct me toward him, and gave me a light kiss.

"That was a first date for the records, thank you," I said.

He rolled his eyes. "I promise the next one will be *safer*; I'd like to make you dinner, and we'll watch a movie at my place." He motioned toward his front door.

"Sounds good to me."

As the head chef at the Inn's restaurant where we worked, I'd get a treat with his cooking. He got out of the van and waved at me, standing on his porch until I backed out of his driveway.

I drove across town to my apartment building and breathed a sigh of relief when I finally opened my door. Bruce, the stray cat I adopted, came running to rub against my legs.

"Hey, sweetie, let's get you a snack," I cooed.

Anticipating dinner, he meowed impatiently while I kicked off my boots and went to the fridge. Bruce greedily took the bits of chicken I held out for him, purring with delight.

Once seated on the couch, I opened Holly's text message. Focusing on the tarot card, I considered its implications. The *Seven of Swords* suggested either theft or betrayal. There was no logical reason to suspect anyone was dishonest with me, so I was convinced the card indicated theft.

Bruce trotted over with one of his toy mice, dropped it at my feet, and mewed. "What's this, buddy?" I picked it up and tossed it.

He took off, pouncing and playing with it. I returned to my phone and concentrated on connecting to my intuition to understand the card. I still felt that the powerful force from the *Seven of Swords* as yet to pass.

Bruce jumped up and dropped the soaking-wet mouse on

my lap. "What the hell, Bruce — you drowned it?" I rubbed his chin, and he purred proudly.

Holly probably wondered what had taken me so long to call her, so I chose the video call. I couldn't visit the covenstead until I completed my journey through the Magic Passage. The High Priestess and the otherworldly entity created this real-time initiation.

"Sophia, there you are," she exclaimed. "I was worried about you."

Even on the phone screen, her smile radiated beauty and power. Her voice was feathery and captivating — I loved to listen to her talk.

"I had one hell of a night. First, my dinner date was interrupted when Louis's sister called and needed a ride. I felt like I was *The Fool* when I pulled a U-turn and wound up in the ditch. Then after binging out on greasy theatre food, we got attacked by robbers in the parking lot." I sighed.

"That's crazy, Sophia. I see you're okay, in any case. How's Louis?"

"His face is a mess. He'll be lucky if his nose isn't broken," I winced.

"Gracious." She brushed her hair back with her fingers. "I'm sure he'll be fine. I'm sensing that Louis is *The fool*."

"I thought it was me," I said.

She laughed. "No, dear; it's Louis. The *Seven of Swords* — representing the present situation, was the incident in the parking lot. The spirit entity wanted you to experience theft."

"I thought so too, but they didn't get away with anything," I said.

"Oh, no?"

"No. Without my talismans, I failed to sense the danger. When I had the chance, as you taught me, I gathered mystical energy and prepared to attack. The crooks got spooked and ran away before I had the chance," I said.

"See? I told you." She smiled proudly.

"Well, I'd love to take the credit, but a couple of girls were coming toward us in the parking lot, and I thought perhaps that's what startled them."

"You don't give yourself enough credit." Holly clicked her tongue disapprovingly. "It was you, Sophia. Your dependence on charms and spells has blinded you to your magical potential. The power is within and all around you. Those objects are just like go-betweens, wasting your energy. Once you complete the Magic Passage, you will understand how competent you are."

"Thank you for your guidance Holly," I said.

"It's my pleasure. This is an exciting time. Things may get a little crazy over the next two days but stay on course. *No cheating.*" She winked exaggeratedly.

"I know — no charms, fetishes, amulets, rituals, spells or any other magical fairy dust." I wiggled my nose at her.

"That's right, only by letting go of those crutches will you be able to graduate to a new class of magic. Then you'll join the crafts elite, and I'll teach you to harness the power of evocation to summon deities." Her eyes grew wide, and pupils dilated until all I could make out were black holes as the amber irises disappeared.

Even through the phone, I could see how excited she was when she discussed higher magic, which made me eager to learn from her. Evocation was a mysterious art and usually required offerings, circle casting, chanting and ceremonies.

Holly taught an ancient technique without the burden of all these things. But first, you had to be reborn through the Magic Passage. It was designed to eliminate the necessity of trinkets to practise a purer form of magic.

"Blessed be," I said.

"Blessed be." Holly ended the call.

I stood in front of the balcony sliding glass door and gazed over the city. The snowflakes twinkled in the light as they fell around the soft glow of the street lamp. I must have been mesmerized because when I looked at the clock — at least an hour had passed since I'd spoken with Holly.

Bruce was asleep in the armchair, and he yawned. It hit me how tired I felt, so I stripped down, brushed my hair, and went to bed.

I blinked and had to squint my eyes against the bright sunlight in my bedroom. How odd; usually, my night was full of vivid dreams rich with imagery and symbolism. My phone started ringing, and I knew it was my mother calling.

"Hi, Mom," I said.

"Sophia, what's going on? I had a terrible dream about you. You were lost in the woods, and no one could find you. Your father told me I was calling for you in my sleep," she said.

"I'm fine, Mom. I was on a date last night, and a couple of muggers tried to steal my purse."

"Oh honey, that's awful. Are you okay?"

"Yes, mom, please don't worry. I'm fine," I assured her.

I didn't want to tell her that Louis was hurt, and I certainly wasn't going to mention the weird trials my High Priestess prepared for my initiation in Sacred Twilight's Fourth Degree.

My mother was a witch like my grandmother before her, and so on. Magic was a part of my family for centuries. My brother Sam and I were introduced to the craft at age four. She was the High Priestess of Golden Crescent; her coven only had three degrees. She disapproved of evocation, claiming it was too dangerous to be beneficial.

"How's Sam?" I changed the subject.

"He's fine; Brenda has him running in circles painting the nursery and taking Lamaze classes. It's good that he owns a landscaping company and doesn't work very much this time of year. I don't know anyone who loves winter more than Sam." She laughed.

My older brother Sam and his wife Brenda announced her

pregnancy almost two weeks ago at our holiday dinner. Dad nearly choked on his turkey, and Mom got so excited that she spilled her wine.

My intercom started to buzz. "I gotta go, Mom — someone's at my door," I said.

"Okay, I'll talk to you soon. I love you."

"Love you too." I hung up.

I pressed the intercom button. "Hello?"

"Your package is here, Ma'am," a young man spoke.

"Okay, I'll be right down."

My phone chimed, and I was acutely aware that Holly had sent another tarot card already. It's like *Grand Central Station*. I haven't even started the coffee maker yet.

I threw on my long winter coat and rushed down four flights to the front entrance. My building was at least eighty years old and had no fancy surveillance systems, so I had to go to the lobby to see who it was.

A young courier waited with a brown box in his hands. I opened the glass door, panting slightly. "Thank you," I said.

He handed me the box. "I noticed the parking spaces are numbered for the units."

"Yeah, not much room for visitors, I know." I shrugged, figuring he was complaining about the lack of parking.

"So, are *you* the owner of the burgundy minivan?" He looked over his shoulder toward my vehicle and pointed at it.

"Yes, why?"

He tilted his head sideways. "Someone flattened all your tires."

"What?" I gasped.

"Yup, *all* of them." He turned and walked toward his truck.

I followed him out the door.

"Good luck, Miss," he said, then got into his delivery vehicle and drove off.

I walked around the van and saw he was right; *all* four tires were slashed. Last night when Holly sent the tarot card, Louis and I were attacked. Today, I received another message, and my tires were flattened.

I hustled back into the building and to my apartment. After locking the door behind me, I hesitantly looked at my phone to see which card Holly had sent. It was *The Prince of Disks*. I called her.

"Hey, babe," she answered cheerily.

"Someone slashed all my tires, Holly," I said in a panicked voice.

"What? Settle down, honey. Remember to ground yourself and breathe."

She was right, of course. It wasn't like me to be this jittery; I took a deep breath and centred myself, imagining a loving universe dancing around me.

"It seems like this entity of yours has a strange way of showing me the path. You sent a text last night, and two thugs tried to rob me. Today, you sent another one, and my tires were slashed."

"Did you call the police?" Holly asked.

"Not yet; I called you first."

"Well, call them and let me know how it goes. The spirit only creates a path; you must travel it. Use your magic and search within yourself. When do you think the tires were vandalized? Just now?"

"No, it couldn't be." I thought back to when the text came. "The delivery guy would've seen it happen and said something."

"Delivery guy?"

"Yeah, I guess the tires could have been damaged anytime last night after I went to bed. I only found out about it because a package came for me," I said.

"What package?" she asked.

"I don't know," I said, looking over at the brown box that Bruce was merrily rubbing up against.

THE PRINCE OF DISKS

"Come on, Bruce, get away from that. You don't know what's in there," I said.

He meowed in response to his name and jumped off the table. Bruce was an orange tabby I found as a kitten when I moved here after college. He was scavenging around the garbage container at the Sandberg Inn; I cleaned him up and brought him home.

"Are you hungry?" I asked.

Coffee took precedence over the tarot card and the mysterious box, so I went into the kitchen to feed Bruce and turn on the brewer. I sniffed the fragrant, earthy aroma of Arabica coffee beans and poured milk into the empty pot ahead of time to be heated.

Even though I thought I slept well, I still felt exhausted. I was asleep as soon as my head hit the pillow and didn't wake up during the night.

Sitting at my kitchenette, I tapped the picture of *The Prince of Disks*. After a sip of my coffee, I concentrated on what and whom this card represented. Nothing came to mind, so following the High Priestess's advice, I closed my eyes and tried again.

Usually, I would have an enchanted object or spell that would have sped this process along. But the whole point of initiation to the Fourth Degree was to awaken my natural powers, naked of magical instruments — like a baby. A metaphysical womb I had to transmigrate to be reborn.

With my eyes closed, finally, images flooded my mind. The immediate influence of this card in the Celtic spread meant that whomever it was, they were affecting me now.

In my mind, I saw a pair of hands with yellow strings tied around each one like a puppeteer. Another image came to me of a pencil and paper. The upturned pencil was frantically erasing something written on it. I focused on the page and saw it was my name.

I opened my eyes and stood up. This vision was a warning. I went into the living room to where I'd left the box and flipped it around to find a return address. There was none, just my name and address printed on a generic label, which could be from anyone. I opened it and to find a bunch of my old belongings.

"What an idiot," I said aloud.

Bruce's attention turned to me from watching snowflakes through the window. I rifled through the package and contemplated how stupid and unnecessary it was to send this package.

It was from my ex-boyfriend Chad. We'd broken up months ago, and he was still bitter about it. The box contained a few things I thought had been thrown out by now. It was clothes, lipstick, conditioner, and a toothbrush.

I couldn't believe he had sent me the dirty toothbrush. I took the lot out of my apartment and dropped it down the garbage shoot.

Instead of calling the police, I decided to call my mechanic to see what he could do. I figured Chad flattened my tires after I told him last week to move on. I wanted him to stop sending me messages and hinted that I had a date.

I pressed Joe's numbers from my contact list.

"Good morning, Joe's Garage," he answered.

"Hi Joe, it's Sophia; how are you?" I said.

"Not bad, Sophia; I'd ask how you were, but it's Saturday morning, and I suspect something's wrong with your van, or you wouldn't be calling me," he said.

"Yeah, someone slashed all my tires last night." I sighed

"Oh my — I'm sorry to hear that. Where were you parked?" he asked.

"In my own parking space at home, I'm guessing it was my ex-boyfriend, so I just want to get it fixed."

"I see; unfortunately, it will cost you a tow truck with a flatbed. I have a guy I can call. The good news is that I have some used tires that will fit your van. I got them cheap online. They're in better shape than yours, and I'll sell them to you for what I paid," Joe said.

"Thank you, Joe. How long do you think it will take?"

"He'll probably pick up your van this morning, and I should be able to squeeze you in early this afternoon," he said.

"Fantastic."

"I'll give Omar your phone number so he can call when he arrives, and you can give him your key."

"Sounds good; I'll talk to you this afternoon. Thanks again."

"No problem, take care," Joe said and hung up.

After talking to Joe, I toasted a sesame seed bagel and slathered it with peanut butter. I let Bruce lick the peanut butter off the plate and finished my coffee. I'd only lived in the city for around a year, and Joe had already serviced my rusty old van at least seven times.

"Time to call Holly back," I said to Bruce.

He shook his head exaggeratedly and wandered off. I tapped her name and selected video chat.

"Hey, doll," she said. "Did you call the police?"

"No, I didn't bother. I called Joe's Garage — he's getting it taken care of soon. The police can't do much anyway. I know who the *Prince of Disks* is," I said.

I watched Holly's reaction as she lifted her left eyebrow quizzically at me. I placed my phone on a stand on the coffee table so she could see my face on the video call without me having to hold my phone.

"Is that right?" she asked.

"It's Chad."

She clapped her hands twice and flashed a big smile at me. "Well done, Sophia. Yes, that's what I sensed as well," she praised.

"Yeah, well, I had a little help figuring that one out, the package that was delivered was a box of my old crap that I'd left behind at his place. I suspect he slashed my tires too — I let it slip a few weeks ago that I had a date." I shook my head and rolled my eyes. "It seemed like a good idea at the time. I thought it would help him to get over our breakup and stop messaging me. Instead, it looks like it set him off," I said.

"You know what to do," she said.

"I suppose it's a little strange to just will him away. I'm so accustomed to using spells for these kinds of problems," I said.

"Think of it like the *force* in *Star Wars*; you don't need props, Sophia — you are the channel for power — not some magical incantations," Holly put her index finger and thumb on her chin and got closer to the camera.

Her eyes were so beautiful, even on the screen. I nodded and thought about what I needed to do to move forward through this element of the Celtic spread. The spirit Holly was using evidently, wanted to challenge me seriously. I expected this would be a fun adventure with a few tests and hadn't foreseen any threats until last night.

"I'll call him," I said.

"You're doing phenomenal, Sophia; what did you do with the personal items in the box?"

My skin prickled, and I had a peculiar feeling of hesitation.

"Oh, I haven't decided yet," I said.

Typically, I would have told her the truth, but something urged me not to. My intuition was fuzzy since starting this initiation, but this feeling was intense.

I'd have to follow my gut; even by not telling Holly the truth, I still followed her directions. She told me to trust myself — that's what I was doing.

"It's up to you, but I think this is a perfect opportunity to practise clearing the objects of negative energy. No incense, bells, salt, candles or stones — just Sophia and her magic," she said while creating a circle in the air with her arms.

I pursed my lips and bowed my head slightly in submission. That seemed to please her because she smiled. She was correct; I could use my magic to be deceptive without using my charms.

My jade sphere of deceit was a small dime-sized ball that I'd enchanted in case I needed to lie. I usually kept it on my keychain, but I managed without it.

"Good idea. I'm going to jump in the shower. I have some errands to run after my van gets fixed."

"Blessed be," Holly said.

"Blessed be."

I threw my pyjamas in the laundry hamper, turned the shower faucet hot, and stepped into the steamy utopia. I longed for my crystals, magic scrubs, and soaps tucked away in Holly's black box.

Holly had replaced it all with a bar of plain scentless soap. A week ago, she came to my apartment and did a complete run-through of my bewitched objects.

Leaving the box here was to ensure I was still *tempted* to use my trinkets but learned to control my dependence on them.

As I washed my hair, I felt the negative energy cascade down my body. I tensed, feeling the power of a banishing spell. I searched around the shower for the culprit but didn't see anything.

Then I noticed the tiles had the faded outline of a soap-drawn symbol I'd created months ago. I let out a long frustrated groan.

I'd used an enchanted vanilla and lavender bar of soap to draw the banishing spell. I thought Holly cleared my apartment thoroughly, but this would be easy to miss. I steered the shower head to the tile wall and used a facecloth to wipe away any remnants of the symbol.

When I got out of the shower to dry off, I had the weird feeling that a heavy cloud suddenly surrounded me. I used my energy to search for a presence, but the feeling faded almost as quickly as it had arrived.

I shrugged it off and got dressed. I needed to carry out the unpleasant task of calling Chad.

Sitting in my comfy armchair, I relaxed and took a few deep, mindful breaths to prepare myself for the conversation. Feeling grounded, I tapped Chad's number and put the phone on speaker.

"Hello," he answered.

"Hi Chad, how are you?"

I reached out to him with magical energy to read his thoughts and intentions. It was so limiting without being able to focus power from an external source; all I could sense was contempt.

"What do you care?" he snapped.

"Come on, don't be like that. Thank you for sending my stuff; you didn't have to do that. I could've picked it up; I didn't realize I'd left anything there."

"I found the clothes mixed in with mine, and the other stuff was underneath the bathroom sink. If you came back, I kept it aside so you would see that I value you. After receiving your last message, I realized *that* was never going to happen," he grumbled.

"What message?"

"You know, the one from a private phone number you sent two days ago. *Hi Chad, please stop messaging me. I've fallen in love with another man — Sophia,*" he said mockingly. "I assumed you were texting from your new boyfriend's phone," he said.

I was confused. I re-centred my mind to see if he was lying. As far as I could tell, he was speaking the truth — or at least he *believed* he was. It made no sense because I didn't send that message.

I took a deep breath, probed a little deeper to find the source of the odd story, and felt a sudden smack of energy. I'd never experienced that before — *Wow, that was freakish.* I felt whiplash from my magic returning to me like that.

"Listen, Chad. I didn't send that message — I don't know who did. What about that girl you went on a couple of dates with, the one you said was obsessed with you?"

"Kelly? No, I see her at the gym; she's got a new guy. So you aren't dating?" He had a bit of hope in his voice.

"Well, I have gone on one date..." I said tentatively.

He interrupted me. "Ptah, maybe your new man sent the message to get rid of *me.*"

"No, he wouldn't do that."

"How do you know? You don't know how people work. You may think you're all that with your *witchy* nonsense, but you don't understand men." Chad said confidently.

We dated for years before I moved to Sandberg, he knew about Golden Crescent, but he still didn't believe in magic. We were high school sweethearts, and after a few years, he became arrogant and cynical, so I no longer found him attractive.

"So you didn't slash my tires?" I probed.

Chad laughed. "Me?" He laughed again. "Check your *new* friends in your city. I'm not a frigging psychopath." He hung up.

I should have known better. Chad may have been the *Prince of Disks*, but he was too self-important to bother skulking around my parking lot and flattening all my tires.

I channelled more psychic energy into the ether, and the image of the men in the balaclavas popped into my head. *They know where I live* — I was filled with fear. I pressed Louis's name on my phone.

"Hi, Sophia; how are you?" Louis said.

"I've been better, and how are you feeling today?"

"Not bad at all. I took a couple of ibuprofen like you suggested and slept like a baby," he answered.

"What are you doing this afternoon?"

"Nothing — until dinner. Then I'm expected at the restaurant. What are you thinking?" he asked.

"Someone flattened my van tires; I'm getting a set of used tires put on. The tow truck should be here any minute. I was hoping you'd give me a ride this afternoon to pick it up when it's ready."

"You're joking?" he exclaimed.

"I wish. Nope, they wrecked them all. I suspect those guys from the theatre — I don't know who else would do that. Maybe they followed me home or something." I said.

"I'll be there in an hour," he said.

THE WORLD

J ended the call with Louis and watched outside for the tow truck. Even with the windows closed, I could hear the massive rig coming. I put my coat on and went down to give Omar my key.

"Good morning, I'm Omar. Joe sent me. I assume this is yours?" Omar pointed at the pitiful-looking van.

"Sadly, yes." I handed him the key.

"You go on inside; I've got this," Omar said, walking away.

"Thank you."

The wind from outside had begun to blow around fiercely, and the warmth from inside comforted me. I didn't envy Omar as I watched him from the lobby hooking chains to my van to lift it and tow it away. *I'm sure I'll be paying a hefty price for that service* — I thought.

Louis showed up not long after, ringing the buzzer. Opening the apartment door, I was delighted he'd brought hot chocolate and donuts.

"These look delicious," I said, noting that they were from a locally owned bakery and not one of the usual franchise coffee shops.

"This is from my favourite place. The baker who works there, Jaiden and I have known each other for years. I went to school with him," he said.

Picking up a cherry cake donut covered with whipped cream, I stuffed it into my mouth. It was *deliciously* moist and sweet with a hint of buttery goodness.

I swallowed it. "I think that is the best thing I've ever tasted." I took another huge bite.

"Whoa, whoa, whoa. I'm going to get jealous — you won't say that after I prepare you a five-course meal." He wiggled his eyebrows.

I was so excited by the baked goodies that I'd temporarily forgotten to inspect his injury. Shockingly, he only had a tiny bruise on the bridge of his nose, and his eyes were okay. I might not have even noticed the mark if I didn't know better.

"What the hell, Louis? You look great," I said.

"Why, thank you." He bowed.

I smacked his shoulder. "That's not what I mean. Your nose — it's almost as if nothing happened."

I got closer and lightly touched the bridge of his nose. He didn't flinch, so I ran my finger up and down to feel if the bone was bumpy or cracked. It was perfectly straight.

"What can I say? I heal quickly. It probably seemed worse than it was — I'm a bleeder."

"I'm glad it isn't bad. I could have sworn you were going to have black eyes," I said, puzzled.

Something about him bewildered me, but I couldn't put my finger on it. Louis was very candid, so I respected him greatly, but I sensed something abnormal that I hadn't before.

My phone chimed; Holly must have pulled another card. The text made me apprehensive — after the last couple of unlucky incidents coinciding with her messages.

Louis took a sip of his hot chocolate. "Who's messaging you?"

I picked up my phone to look like I didn't know who it was. "It's Holly; I'll call her later."

The tarot card on the banner was visible; it was *The World*. This would be the fourth card in the spread indicating the near future—some short-term effects resulting from my immediate actions.

This was a pain in the butt. I had to go through the trial while continuing my life as if I wasn't facing a huge undertaking.

"I'm surprised you didn't call her instead of me." Louis tilted his head, scrutinizing me.

"Holly has the flu; until she feels better, she's staying close to home," I rehearsed the story Holly instructed me to tell people in case anyone asked for her.

Evoking the spirit to manifest in and manipulate the physical world required Holly's undivided attention. While I traversed through the Magic Passage, she would spend time keeping track of the unearthly entity; doing this required powerful magic.

"I was hoping you called me because you had such a fabulous time last night and couldn't wait to see me again," Louis smirked. "I suspected *you* slashed your tires as an excuse to get me to come over."

"Oh right," I put my palm on my forehead. "You got me. I figured I needed new tires anyway, and playing the *damsel in distress* is my favourite game."

He laughed. "Hey, kitty, you want some whipped cream?"

Bruce was purring loudly and rubbing against his legs. Louis was wearing his black casual pants that were part of his uniform at the restaurant, and my cat was leaving his orange and white fur all over them.

"Oh crap. Bruce, stop it," I scolded. "Sorry, Louis."

"Don't worry; it'll wipe off. My parents have a cat too." He put a little whipped cream on his finger and let Bruce lick it off.

While he was preoccupied with my cat, I considered *The*

World card. This one was pretty obvious. Holly was teaching me to use my supernatural abilities to influence the world around me using the energy from the quantum realm.

The problem for me was that it was too chaotic and unpredictable. All these unlucky incidents were entirely out of my control. I felt blinded because I didn't foresee any of it. *The World* also pointed to the end of an era and the beginning of another one.

"So when are we going to set up our second date anyway?" he asked.

"Whenever you'd like."

He stroked his chin thoughtfully. "How about Monday when we're both off work? I'm cooking dinner, and I'll make sure Katie isn't in town."

"Monday's good. Are you sure you can get Katie to go home?" I lifted my eyebrows doubtfully.

"She won't get a choice. Plus, nothing fun for a teenage girl is happening on a *Monday*. No interruptions this time." He smiled.

It was strange to date Louis. He was a great friend, and I felt confident he would be a sweet boyfriend. Unfortunately, I was distracted by hiding the truth that I was a witch.

I needed to find a way to consolidate and figure out how to make it work. Holly told me that's why she didn't have a partner and preferred the company of a *few* lovers.

Ironically it would be easier to hide my magic from Louis and others by learning to craft it without all the fluff. I would miss my magical charms but using a higher form of natural magic meant I didn't need them.

"I'm not sure how long my van will take. I wonder if I should call the police and tell them my tires were slashed. I thought it was my ex-boyfriend at first, but he made it clear he couldn't be bothered, and I believe him," I said, feeling my cheeks get hot with embarrassment.

Louis pulled out the card the detective gave him and handed

it to me. "Call now; tell Detective Connelly that we met last night. I'm sure he'll send a car around the neighbourhood periodically to keep an eye out," Louis said.

I took Joseph Connelly's card and dialled the number. The detective didn't answer, so I left a voicemail and the incident number assigned to the assault from the previous night. Feeling a little better, I saw Louis walking around my apartment, looking at my stuff.

"Where are all your magical instruments, Sophia?" he asked.

I was confounded and needed a second to process. "I'm sorry; what did you say?"

"Your crystal ball was here before." He pointed at my desk. "You had amulets hanging over the window. You aren't wearing your silver moon necklace, and your bookshelf is near empty." His eyebrows furrowed.

Relax, Sophia. He doesn't know you're a witch — I said to myself. Louis had been to my apartment once before, briefly when my van broke down and Holly was out of town.

I'd called him for a ride to work. He came up for a few minutes while I took on a call from Sam about dinner plans for Mom's birthday. He would've had time to look around and see my magical tools. Many people are interested in magic, but it doesn't mean they know how to use it.

I waved my hands in the air dismissively. "Oh, you know, I grew out of that stuff. Time to move on."

The World tarot card entered my mind again, and I interpreted the meaning. The end of this era and progress to the next — I needed to discard my beloved magical instruments.

I couldn't keep witchcraft a secret from guests with charms and talismans on display — too much evidence. It was only a one-bedroom apartment, with no room to create a separate sacred space for my rituals and altar.

"I don't think so," he said speculatively. Looking all around, he stopped to stare at my ceiling. "I'm sensing more mystical energy than the last time I was here. I'm not sure what's going on yet, but this place is full of mysterious power. I can taste it," Louis said.

I could feel that my eyebrows had risen high on my forehead, and my eyes were bulging. "Excuse me?" I blurted.

I could barely fathom what he was insinuating. *He did know!* I was confounded. *How is this possible?* My mind raced. He'd have to have been aware of witchcraft, realized I was practising it, and hidden these facts from me.

He was a witch too, and I missed it. Holly warned me that my magic was weak and ineffective when she told me I had more to learn.

"No sense playing games; I know Holly and the Sacred Twilight coven have you wrapped around their fingers," Louis said, crossing his arms.

I gulped. "You're a witch?"

"Yes, I belong to a small coven, Lunar Pyre, from Henmount." He sat down on my chair and motioned for me to do the same.

"How is it that I didn't know that?" I asked, shaking my head.

He reached into the front of his shirt and pulled out his necklace. Dangling on end was a beautiful amulet. A pentagram with a circle around it and a small crescent moon in the middle with the points facing up like horns. It reminded me of the symbol from my mother's coven, Golden Crescent. With my necklace put away, I felt a pang of envy seeing his charm.

"I'm using a dynamic lunar invisibility spell to keep *you* and that *sow* Holly from manipulating me. Looking around your apartment, I see *you're* the one getting exploited." Louis sighed.

"I'm so confused right now," I said, scrambling to collect and control my powers to help me decide what I should or shouldn't say. He knew about Sacred Twilight and didn't seem to have the appreciation for Holly and her abilities that I did.

"I know you are. That's one of the ways she catches people in her web," he scoffed.

"Web?" I put my fingers on both my temples. I felt foggy and couldn't concentrate. *What in the hell is he talking about?* Unable to summon any magic, I just sat there helplessly, waiting for Louis to continue.

"Yeah, she's like a spider who weaves her dark magic around unsuspecting witches so that she can manipulate and control them," he said.

"That's not true, Louis." I'd had it with him insulting Holly. Perhaps he was the one using dark magic. After all, it wasn't until I went on a date with him that all the unlucky events started happening. *He* was the one who told me to turn around, causing us to get stuck in the ditch. I decided to approach the situation cautiously.

"Listen to me, Sophia," he said, putting his hands on my shoulders and staring me in the eye. I felt the electricity of his touch and could feel myself consume his energy like the empty tank of a car at the pump that was getting fuelled up.

He ripped his hands away from me with an expression of horror on his face.

"What happened?" I asked.

I could sense his power, and the thick murkiness in my head had cleared. It felt wondrous, like recovering from a cold virus. The sensation didn't last; a haze clung to me like a nebula.

"You've been mesmerized," he said. "Not only that but she's cursed you or something. Your magic isn't with you." He looked puzzled.

"Where is it?"

"I don't know, but you're weaker than yesterday. When I touched you just now, you absorbed my magic. Involuntarily I'm sure; I'm not accusing you of anything. I know she did something to you."

"Accusing me?" I lost it. "How do *I* know it's not *you* using dark magic? You hid the fact that you're a witch from me — for a year now." I started to pace around the room. "I mean, this all started when you asked me out; all of a sudden, my powers are weak. We both know there is no such thing as coincidences." I glared at him.

"First of all, we both hid the truth from each other. The difference is that I had a reason to, but you've been dazzled into hiding your magic by Sacred Twilight. I don't blame you, though. Holly's the High Priestess of a dangerous dark magic cult, and you're her next victim."

"*I am not*," I interrupted. For some reason, my voice didn't sound as convincing as I wanted. "Holly's my best friend, and she's teaching me higher magic."

"Why all the secrecy?" Louis demanded.

"Well…" I stuttered. "Some people frown upon magic. Being judged constantly for our beliefs is why we don't parade around flaunting it," I said defensively.

"That sounds paranoid," he said.

"No, it's not. My ex-boyfriend made fun of my witchcraft. I levitated his baseball, and he laughed. He said he watched a guy on YouTube do that, and it's trickery." I sniffed.

"She slowly convinced you her way of magic is superior to others with her elitist attitude. Now it looks like you've been isolated from the other members of your coven. She's a wicked vixen using dark magic to convince you to follow her," he said.

I was getting pissed off. How dare he say those things. Of course, he's wrong. I didn't believe Holly could work with dark magic; she urged us to steer clear of it. Even from the start, when I met her, I felt loving energy.

"Why would she do that? I asked.

"To cannibalize your magic," Louis answered.

NINE OF CUPS

I was livid. Even with my magic weakened, such as it was, I could sense that Louis was being honest with me. The problem was that I couldn't trust myself because I'd missed so much. Louis was a witch, and I'd been working with him for over a year and didn't even know it.

I'd fallen victim to somebody's lies, that was certain. Being mad wouldn't help; anger would only hinder my abilities more. I promptly forgave myself and thanked the universe for the valuable lesson.

"What you're saying is ridiculous. We're witches, not vampires." I rolled my eyes.

"I'm not talking about mythological monsters. Holly's dangerous, and you know it. Think about it — where are all your candles? I'll show you," he said.

I didn't want him to jeopardize my initiation into the Fourth Degree. "They're put away."

"No wonder you're so weak. Don't you feel strange?" he asked.

"Well, sort of, but I'm not convinced that it isn't your doing." I stood up and went into my kitchen to get away from him for a moment to clear my head. The atmosphere was like pea soup, and I couldn't summon any magic.

"Did Holly give you a black box?" Louis asked, calling out from the living room.

I turned sharply and marched back to stand in front of him. We were the same height, so I glared straight into his green eyes. "How do *you* know so much about Sacred Twilight?"

He stared back at me without flinching. "Before you came along, my cousin Shelley was their thirteenth member. Last year she mysteriously disappeared, and no one has seen or heard from her. Then, *you* replaced her."

I was taken aback. The way he said it sounded accusing. "You don't think I had anything to do with her disappearance?"

"Not anymore, but I did at first." He nodded.

Feeling offended, I raised my voice. "I had nothing to do with it. Shelley was gone before Holly approached me, and I was told she'd moved on because she had higher aspirations."

"I believe you, Sophia. It would be best if you believed me when I tell you this — you're in *danger*. Holly isn't who you think she is. That black box, where is it? We found one in Shelley's apartment after she went missing. It had all her handwritten spellbooks, candles, crystals, soaps — you name it. If it was imbued with magic, it was in the box." Louis put his hands on his hips as he scanned the room, looking for it.

My phone rang. I answered, and Joe told me the van was ready to be picked up.

"My van's fixed; I can't stand being stranded. Are you going to drive me still?" I asked.

"Of course; that's why I'm here," he said.

"Oh, I wasn't sure anymore; I feel I've been played. I thought you were interested in me, but you've been hiding your ulterior motivations."

The realization that Louis was possibly dating me to get

information on his missing cousin or dirt on Holly hurt. I liked him a lot and felt disappointed.

"I asked you out despite my suspicions, Sophia. The only thing that has changed is that I'm even more invested in finding out what happened to my cousin. Not just because I care about her, I care about you too. I'm worried about what's happening here and what Holly's planning to do to you," he said.

"I need to think. Please drop me off at the mechanics so I can get my van." I sighed.

Louis put his shoes on. "Let's go."

Outside was still windy; it looked like a blizzard was starting. When I slipped on the ice again, I nearly landed flat on my ass, but he caught me.

I speculated that he was using his magic to trip me. I feared he was right about Sacred Twilight but didn't want to tell him about the trials. He could be part of the plan for my initiation; I wasn't sure.

We got into his hatchback, and he drove carefully on the snow-covered roadway. "Do yourself a favour and take your possessions out of that cursed box."

"I don't know what you mean." I avoided looking at him and watched the snowflakes whipping around in the wind.

"Yes, you do. Search inside yourself and seek the truth."

I shifted uncomfortably in my seat and changed the subject. "So, I assume you used a healing spell to fix your nose?"

He nodded. "That's right."

"Why didn't you sense those thugs last night? If I'm cursed, that would explain why I didn't feel the source of the danger, but what about *you*?" I challenged.

"That's an excellent point. I've been asking myself the same question. Those guys had to have magical assistance to cloak themselves from me — or us."

"I did have a bad feeling in the washroom, but I couldn't feel where it originated," I admitted.

"Better than me; I didn't suspect anything. They caught me completely off guard. That concerns me; please be careful, Sophia." His eyes flicked toward me quickly and then back to the road.

"I'll be fine."

Louis pulled into the parking lot of Joe's Garage and parked the car. He put his arm behind my chair and leaned toward me. At first, I thought he would try to kiss me, and I almost slapped him.

"I finish at ten — we need to talk. Will you call me later tonight? " he asked.

He seemed genuinely concerned. My emotions were confusing — I wanted to date Louis, *the chef*. I didn't know who Louis *the witch* was.

I wasn't convinced his low opinion of Holly, and Sacred Twilight was justified. I didn't dare tell him about the Magic Passage. I feared he would react like a bloodhound and interfere.

"I'll call. Thanks for the ride," I said.

I got out of the car and slammed the door in case he thought to say anything else. I needed to clear my head and determine the best course of action.

My phone vibrated in my pocket when I rushed into the building to escape the chilly gusts of snow. The familiar chime was faint, but I recognized that Holly had sent another tarot card.

Joe was on the phone when I walked into the entryway. While waiting for him, I pulled my phone out of my pocket to see the card. It was the *Nine of Cups*. As the fifth card of the Celtic spread, this card represented the past. It was a card of getting what you thought you wanted but didn't make you feel the way you expected.

"Howdy Sophia, You ready for the damage?" Joe asked.

"Not really, but let's see it anyway."

He handed me the bill. "Here you go; that's the best I could do."

I took the bill from him and looked directly at the bottom right-hand corner. The total was four hundred and twenty-nine dollars.

"That includes the tow?" I asked, flipping the page to see the other side.

"Yes, Omar felt sorry for you and gave you a little discount."

I reached into my purse for my wallet. "That's great. Thank you, Joe, and thank Omar for me too. I'll pay by credit card."

Once the bill was paid, I felt better. Especially when I got behind the wheel of my vehicle, even though it had only been half a day. I preferred the freedom to drive wherever I wanted without depending on anyone. Independence was something I valued highly.

Autonomy was important to Sacred Twilight; they didn't have a permanent covenstead to get together. The High Priestess often gave us directions to different addresses where she'd arranged for us to gather, practice magic, and perform rituals.

She boasted that we were uninhibited and could go anywhere without the burden of boundaries like other covens.

The drive to the grocery store was extremely slippery. I wanted to get home and call Holly, but first, I needed to pick up a few things, including cat litter for Bruce. Summoning magic to bump up to first in the line at the grocery store was usually simple.

This time I needed to tighten the muscles in my forearms as I straightened my fingers, then balled my fists. Finally, a teenager appeared at the check-out with the closed sign.

He waved at me. "I can help you over here."

I turned my cart from the back of a line and checked out. After I put everything in the van, I got in, started the engine, and called Holly.

"Sophia, there you are," she chirped.

"Hey, Holly," I said.

"You're phoning me from your van; I'm happy you fixed it so quickly," she said. "You've seen *The World*. What does that mean to you?"

"It's the card of the past and getting what one wants. I'm feeling the freedom to perform magic anywhere without the use of my magical toolbox. Liberation from dependence on external objects. It also comes with a price that I didn't expect." I said.

"Mhmm, what kind of price, Sophia?"

"My withdrawals from being able to use my charms and spells are a lot stronger than I'd anticipated," I said.

"That makes sense," she said. "Anything else? I'm sensing more."

"Brace yourself for this one. Louis is a witch, he knows about Sacred Twilight, and he suspects you're using *dark magic* to manipulate me," the words poured out of me effortlessly. I wasn't sure what I would say until I said it.

She laughed heartily like I'd told her some great joke. "That's wondrous; the spiritual entity has given you amazing challenges."

"I'm surprised you aren't upset. He *knows* about Sacred Twilight and accused you of black magic." I repeated cautiously.

"Shelley — your predecessor was Louis's cousin. His family is upset that she up and moved away without saying goodbye. They've blamed us for her disappearance since the beginning. Her family is extremely dysfunctional. The Lunar Pyre members resented that Shelley started dating a member of our coven and decided to join us," Holly said.

"Really? Who did she date?"

"Jamie," she said.

"I didn't know that."

She sighed. "No, I don't suspect Louis told you *that* information. He's imagined Sacred Twilight as the villain for some time now. I don't know whether it's jealousy or concern for his family, but be careful. Those negative emotions blind him, and his magic will be contaminated, giving him a skewed sense of reality."

"I can't believe you didn't tell me all this before; you knew I was going on a date with him," I said.

"You must learn to use *your magic* to discover the dangers around you, Sophia. This initiation is designed to help you," she said.

"So there's no dark magic influence in my life; why do I feel surrounded by a heavy fog?"

"What do your instincts tell you?" she asked.

My instincts told me to *watch my back*, and I couldn't trust her more than I could trust Louis. Until this dense haze suppressing my magic lifted, I wanted to be careful. It almost felt like my inner powers had been clogged.

Holly was the most powerful witch I'd ever encountered. If she had any malicious intent — I needed to be wary. Otherwise, she's genuinely guiding me through the Magic Passage for spiritual growth to gain the valuable experience I desire. Perhaps it was Louis that I needed to worry about.

"My instincts are telling me to put a better guard up," I said.

"Excellent, Sophia, and what about the *Nine of Cups*?"

"In the past, even though I used all my magic possessions and spells — I still *missed* that Louis was a witch. I only discovered he was hiding his ability when I had no tools. The card tells me I've enjoyed some satisfaction from the past, but I'll receive what I truly desire in the future," I said.

"Yesss," Holly cheered like I'd scored a goal in hockey. "Your progress is magnificent, Sophia. The entity is guiding you, and soon you'll have full control. We'll talk very soon."

"Before you hang up, do you think this spiritual entity manifested is creating this heavy feeling I have?"

"The being is creating the circumstances in the physical

world to challenge you. The heavy feeling you have is the *withdrawal* of not having the assistance of magic instruments. It's a necessary step toward higher magic. I explained this before," she said.

"I know; I'm just astonished at how wearisome the symptoms are. I feel like my magic has been so unresponsive." I huffed.

"I understand. I went through the same thing when my High Priest, John, initiated me into the Fourth Degree. I found it excruciating to use magic without the elements around me in favour of the deeper power hidden in the quantum realm. If it were easy, all witches could control this power. But I will tell you what John told me — *you are a child of divine light, and the power is within you.*"

"Blessed be," I said.

"Blessed be." She hung up.

I was almost home, and although the wind had settled down a bit, the snow was falling heavily, and visibility was deteriorating.

I grabbed my little two-wheel grocery cart and filled it. Without it, there was no way I could carry all my groceries and the big bag of cat litter up flights of stairs in one trip, lacking the full use of my magic.

I locked the van and closed my eyes to focus on protecting it from future harm. With no spell — I envisioned a force field around the truck. Then, blinking away the snowflake lingering in my eyelashes, I hauled my cart inside to the warmth.

"Hi Bruce, how's my good kitty?" I reached down and scratched his chin while he rubbed against my boots, meowing.

With groceries put away, I decided to meditate. Usually, I'd light candles, play soft relaxing music and sit in front of my altar. Instead, I resolved to sit cross-legged on the living room floor and attempt to channel energy without familiar ritual preparations.

I focused on clearing the room of the dark energy mist surrounding me. I barely had the chance to take one deep breath before something dropped on my lap.

"Okay, Bruce, am I going to do this in my bedroom?" I asked.

I opened my eyes, picked up the soft object my cat gifted me, and inspected it.

FIVE OF WANDS

"*W*here in the world did you get this?" The purring fuzzball crawled onto my lap and started kneading my thighs to soften them for his nap.

He was happily settled, so I stayed seated on the floor while he cuddled into a sleeping position and closed his eyes.

Everyone knows cats are famous for interrupting people who are preoccupied. Curiosity and desire for affection encourage this unmannerly behaviour.

"I haven't seen this for months. I thought it fell off my keychain or something. Where have you been hiding this, buddy?" I stroked Bruce's fur.

He yawned, looked toward my closet door, then tucked his head into himself so that he looked like a ball.

I held the charm but was prohibited from having the enchanted item and needed to put it away. Bruce was so adorable and cozy that I figured a couple of minutes wouldn't hurt, so I just sat there.

The rabbit's foot was a gift from my brother; it was my favourite colour — a rich dark purple.

I sniffed it, wondering what the odd smell was. I pulled it

away from my face and guessed it must have been hiding inside a shoe or boot for the last few months.

My fingers started to tingle, and I could feel the power inside the rabbit's foot enter my hand and travel up my arm into my body.

This was a new experience as I'd never been denied the use of magic-imbued objects before this initiation.

I could almost understand the battle of a person who suffered from drug addiction. I found it nearly impossible to put the rabbit's foot down first.

Then the magic was gone; I'd absorbed it. Same as when Louis touched me this morning. It was like I'd become a vortex to oblivion; instead of becoming stronger with magic, I was being drained.

I inspected the rabbit's foot again — it was empty. I carefully lifted Bruce off my lap, gingerly placed him on the couch, and put the rabbit foot on my desk. *Time for some research.* I called my mother.

"Hi, sweetie, how are you?" she answered.

"Oh, not too bad and you?" I asked.

"Good, I'm just working at the craft fair; they needed volunteers," she said.

I knew she loved going to the craft fair. They held quarterly events, and all the little towns had vendors who would take turns setting up. I could hear the pleasure in her voice and didn't want to distract her.

"I was calling to see what you planned to buy for Brenda's baby shower. Perhaps we could go in on something together," I suggested.

I changed my mind about asking her about a missing girl from Sacred Twilight. She was a High Priestess and knew I was in a secretive coven, but she didn't interfere or question the rites and rituals of other covens. I decided to settle for the internet.

"We could do that. I was planning on getting a crib, a mobile and a basket filled with various baby goodies. While I'm here, I'll pick up a few things. What's your budget?"

"I just dropped over four hundred bucks in my van, so how about you let me pay for the basket, and you and Dad can give them the crib and mobile?"

"Oh dear, that van is a money pit," she chuckled. "I'll take care of the basket and put your name on it, don't worry, honey," she said.

"I'll shoot you some cash when I see you. Thanks, Mom."

"Is there anything else?" she asked.

I could hear the crowd's murmur in the background and decided not to burden her and let her enjoy herself. "That's it, have fun. Love you."

"Love you too," she said and hung up.

I sat at my little desk and opened my laptop to search the internet for the mysterious disappearance of this missing coven-mate, Shelley.

I didn't know her last name but finding a newspaper article didn't take long. The first headline read — *Woman vanishes*.

I read the featured article about Shelley Dorn. Louis's last name was Nelson. I could see after reading the clipping that Shelley's mother and Louis's mother were sisters.

A few months later, there was another news story about how the family suspected foul play, but the local police dismissed the investigation because of a lack of evidence.

I reread the stories twice and reflected on what they said.

Shelley worked at the Café that Louis frequented — the one he brought me donuts and hot chocolate from. Interviews with her co-workers said she was friendly and polite and that they couldn't understand why she disappeared.

Shelley's mother told the reporter that her daughter would never vanish and that something terrible must've happened. She described a happy young woman with a bright future and a loving, supportive family that she visited often.

It made no sense. She had a boyfriend at the time who was interviewed, and his name was Jamie Schneider. No one else in Sacred Twilight was mentioned in either write-up; Jamie was cleared as a suspect in the investigation.

I stared at the picture of Shelley on my computer screen. Using my psychic ability, I tried to see if I could understand her situation or get an impression of her whereabouts.

I had a clear image of fire. Then suddenly, the air around me thickened, and I couldn't sense anything at all — it was like being underwater.

I scrolled through my contacts and tapped Jamie's name.

He answered on the first ring. "Why are you calling me?"

"Hi Jamie, I wanted to ask you a couple of questions," I said, noticing my call put him off.

"The rules are clear, Sophia. During initiation to the Fourth Degree, you're not supposed to talk to covenmates. The Magic Passage is yours alone to travel. I can't help you." He hung up.

I sat back in my chair, stunned. I was going to tell him it wasn't a question about the Magic Passage; it was about his ex-girlfriend, but he ended the call before I had the chance to explain.

Usually, Jamie was polite and friendly, but Holly ran a tight ship, so perhaps he was concerned about that.

Feeling wiped out, I hoped that maybe I'd feel refreshed after a nap. Dragging myself to the bedroom, I pulled the black-out blinds down, crawled under my soft quilt, and flopped my head on the pillow.

The phone chime woke me up. Holly's familiar jingle meant that she'd sent another card already.

I picked up my phone to notice that only an hour had passed. The tarot card was the *Five of Wands*.

My head was groggy; I felt worn out instead of renewed. I

stared at the sixth card of the Celtic spread — a card about the future. My ideals and goals should be understood.

This card meant that constructive energy was being used negatively—the desire for destruction — another warning. The phone rang.

"Hello." I held my phone above my head because I was still lying in bed, so Holly.

"You're in bed?"

"I'm feeling spent; I went for a little snooze," I smiled weakly at her.

"I'm not surprised. Did you see the card?" Holly asked.

"I did," I said.

"And?" She probed.

"I'm not sure; I just woke up," I chucked.

"You need to get up and start focusing. The *Five of Wands* should explain why you're so weak. You've been carrying on with some counterproductive activities," she said.

Dammit, that bugger Jamie ratted me out.

"I can explain," I said.

"Please do."

"I was curious about Shelley. I wanted to convince Louis that he was way off base with his accusations against *Sacred Twilight*. I searched online for articles, and because Jamie used to date her, I wanted to ask him about what had happened. He hung up on me before I had the chance to explain." I shrugged.

"Well, Jamie knows better than to interfere with a coven-mates degree initiation. It doesn't matter what you want to talk about — the rules are clear. No contact with the coven until initiation is completed. If you have any questions — you talk to me," she snipped.

"My apologies, Holly," I said.

I was almost at the point where I didn't care anymore about the Fourth Degree. Holly warned me that I'd only get one shot at it, but I'd been happy before all this started.

47

I questioned whether or not I wanted to use magic without my instruments.

"I know you're thinking about quitting, and that's to be expected; you're at a difficult point in the process. You must persevere, Sophia; I promise it will be worth it." Holly said soothingly.

It was like she could read my mind. "Okay, I'm getting up."

"Good girl, now make yourself something to eat and prepare for a tough night. You need to build your power for the Goddess, and she will replenish your energy and strengthen your magic," she said.

"Thank you, Holly."

"Blessed be." She hung up.

It was a full moon, and I was expected to perform the beautiful and powerful rite of *Drawing down the Moon*. Holly had a unique way of invoking the Goddess and directed me to execute her instructions at midnight.

She advised me to expect a highly altered consciousness when the Goddess appropriated my body.

I got up out of bed and ran myself a nice bubble bath. I may not have access to my elixirs, but I did have some dish soap.

I felt slightly optimistic when I entered the kitchen, where I put away the detergent I'd purchased at the grocery store. Lovely — *french lavender.*

I turned the hot faucet on full and the cold enough, so I didn't scald myself. Tipping the bottle over the running water, I squeezed about one-third into the tub. The aromatic bouquet was divine, and I breathed it in deeply through my nose, feeling instantly lighter.

Holly would have scolded me for this, but *I didn't enchant* the soap. Although she forbade the use of any fragrance, I indulged in this minor indiscretion anyway.

Soaking in the bath for more than half an hour made me feel blissful. I dried off with my softest towel and dressed in a smooth-flowing cotton gown that I could quickly shed later when performing the ritual during the full *Snow Moon*.

I prepared a tuna casserole to put in the oven, which drove Bruce crazy, and he meowed frantically until I offered him a little of the fish.

Afterward, he ran around the room, attacking his toys like a boss. When my phone rang, I'd just finished mixing the boiled noodles with the shredded cheese, cream, peas and tuna.

"Hi, Louis," I said.

"Hi Sophia, I was thinking and wanted to apologize for my behaviour. Would it be all right if I come over later?" Louis asked.

"It's a full moon, Louis. There is no sense in lying to you; I have plans tonight." I said.

"I won't take up much of your time, I promise. I can get out of here an hour early, and I thought you might like it if I brought you a piece of the chocolate mousse pie I just finished making for the restaurant."

"Chocolate mousse?"

He laughed. "That's right. I know you're going to love it."

The sound of his laughter tugged at my heart, plus I loved chocolate, and he knew it. "Oh, you know my weakness. Fine, but you can't stay long. I'm drawing down the moon tonight," I said, knowing that, as a fellow witch, he understood.

"I figured it was something like that. Don't worry; I'll only drop in for dessert, then leave you to it," he said.

After the relaxing bath and the smell of casserole in the oven, I was in a good mood. "Okay, Louis. I'll see you later."

"You won't regret it," he assured me and hung up.

"We'll see," I said to the air.

I fed the cat and ate the casserole, deliberating on the last day's events. Crazy things had happened, but I thought everything would work out soon. I could focus on my new abilities and begin the new normal.

The casserole was delicious initially, but by the time I got to the last bite, it had a pasty flavour, and the room felt heavy again. The negative energy was palpable, and I couldn't clear it away.

I looked at Bruce sitting on the floor, regarding me quizzically. "You feel that, Bruce?" I asked.

He turned slowly and purposefully and trotted toward the living room, looking behind me, beckoning me to follow.

Why not? — I thought and got up to see where he went. He entered the living room, jumped up on the coffee table, and stared directly at the ceiling fan.

"What's up there?" I asked.

Jumping off the table, Bruce started to bat something around on the floor that looked too small to be one of his toys. I walked over to pick the object up and recognized it as a cheap dollar-store birthday candle.

"How did you get that?" I laughed.

I returned to the kitchen to put it in the junk drawer so he wouldn't get sick from chewing the wax.

Opening the drawer, my attention was drawn to a single matchstick. It must have slipped out of the box when Holly took the fire implements and put them in the onyx chest.

Bruce was at my feet again, looking up at me, and he let out a single meow. "You're going to get me in trouble, little fella," I said.

I sat at the kitchen table and focused on the match so that it lit automatically. *Good, at least I still have that ability.* I took the matchstick, lit the little yellow birthday candle, and gazed at the flame.

I looked deep into the fire element with a question — *What do you want to show me?* The answer came quickly, and I saw Shelley with an agonizing expression on her face, burning in the fire.

FULL MOON

I washed the dishes and cleaned every room in the apartment. By the time I was finished, it was around eight-thirty, and Louis would be showing up soon.

Retrieving the black obsidian box from underneath my bed, where Holly had tucked it away, I placed it on the table.

I didn't watch her collect my things, so I wasn't sure what was there. The larger items she took away, like my spell books, potions, candles, and crystal ball.

After the vision I had of Shelley looking tormented, it was undeniable that Holly was deceiving me. Especially after Louis asked me if I had a black box — in magic, coincidences are anything but.

I wanted to open it before he arrived; I didn't know if I could trust *him*, although I was leaning that way.

The obsidian must have powerful magic attached to it because I felt uneasy handling the smooth chest. I attempted to unhook the latch to lift the lid, but it didn't budge.

Frustrated, I put it on the floor and tried to hold the bottom down with my feet while attempting to lift the top open. Nothing still...

I grabbed a knife from the kitchen and tried to shove it between the lid and the bottom to pry it open, but it wouldn't penetrate between the upper and lower halves.

I was upset that I couldn't get the damn box open. I'd have to wait for Louis to show up and see if he could help me. I attempted to use my magic, but it felt like the more I willed it to open, the more it resisted my magic.

Struggling with the complexity of the locking spell exhausted me. I gave up and turned on the television to find that the Weather Channel had issued a severe weather alert.

The statement described blizzard conditions that included heavy snow and frequent gusts of wind above sixty kilometres per hour. Reduced visibility would cause lousy driving conditions.

My intercom buzzer went off shortly after nine o'clock, and I pressed the button. "Come on up, Louis."

"Thank you."

I heard his boots squeaking down the hall and opened the door for him ahead of time. "Ooh, you look like a popsicle."

"It's cold out there, and the heater in my car is crap." He shivered.

He was carrying two bags, one paper and another plastic one. I took them from him and set them on the counter while he took his coat off.

Bruce was pleased to have a house guest because he rubbed himself against Louis's boots, purring. I peeked inside the paper bag to see a plastic container.

"Oh, you *do* have an obsidian box," Louis exclaimed. Passing by it when he followed me into the kitchen. "Have you opened it yet?"

"I tried," I shrugged. "Holly's conjured some powerful spell that has it locked up tight. My magic didn't work; it felt like a Russian doll. When I thought I had it, there's another layer and so on."

Louis returned to the living room, picked up the box, and inspected it. "Interesting. It's identical to the one we found at Shelley's place."

"Can you open it?" I asked.

"Perhaps, but first," he put it on the coffee table. "I owe you an apology and a slice of my world-famous chocolate pie."

I lifted an eyebrow at him. "World-famous, eh?"

"You'll see. Where are your plates?" he asked.

He opened the paper bag in the kitchen and pulled out the disposable container. I grabbed the dishes, and he levitated the two slices of delicious-looking pie onto the plates.

I chuckled. "Show off."

I grabbed a couple of treats for Bruce because chocolate wasn't good for cats, and it didn't seem nice to eat the savoury dessert without giving him a little snack.

I took a bite, and an intense burst of soft creamy chocolate filled my tastebuds.

"Oh my god," I said, driving my fork in for another mouthful.

He winked at me. "That's what everyone says when they try my delectables."

I laughed. "Such a comedian."

"So am I forgiven?"

I washed the plates and turned to look at him. "I'm not upset with you, Louis. Something's wrong — I want to know what it is. I should tell you that I summoned a vision of Shelley earlier."

"Really?"

"Yeah, it was grim, I'm afraid. Something happened to her, but my magic is so weak I can't seem to be able to muster up any other visions."

"You should be able to access some of your abilities now," Louis said.

I felt different. "What did you put in the mousse?" I asked suspiciously.

"A little consecrated water, some black salt, and a few other homemade banishing herbs," he said.

"I can't believe it. Did she *curse* me?" I marched into the living room and picked up the box.

"As soon as you open it, she's going to know. I will bet she's tethered herself to you or the chest," Louis said.

I put it down. "You're right; I can sense that some of my magic is functioning now. Her presence here is so thick that I can practically smell her French perfume."

"You can?" he asked.

"Yeah, you can't?"

"Holly is damn near invisible to me — her whole coven is. When my family went after them for Shelley's disappearance, they pulled some heavy-duty disguising spell." Louis paced around my small living room as he spoke.

"No one in Lunar Pyre can pick up any of Sacred Twilight's magic. We even reached out to another coven that had run-ins with the previous High Priest — John. They couldn't sense magic from the coven either. They've managed to keep themselves cloaked from other witches — except you, of course."

"I'm wondering about the assault at the theatre. You didn't sense the danger," I said.

"I didn't." He confirmed.

"I had a foreboding premonition in the washroom but ignored it because I was trying not to use magical aids," I said.

"So you sensed danger briefly, and you can sense Holly now. Do you think it's possible that your covenmates attacked us?" Louis asked.

"I'm unable to rule it out. Who else would target us? Now that we're dating and knowing your history with the coven, I'm very suspicious." I folded my arms protectively.

"We need to get ahead of them." Louis sat down on the couch, put his elbows on his knees, and rested his chin in his hands.

"I think you should open it." I patted the shiny black chest. "I want my stuff out of there. We can come up with some excuse for why you opened it."

"Like what?" Louis asked.

"We had a fight, and you opened it to make a point, so I kicked you out." I smiled.

"How dramatic, Sophia," he said, smiling.

"Mhmm. Open it." I rubbed my hands together.

Bruce strolled in and stood near the box; apparently, he wanted it open too.

Louis brought the plastic bag from the kitchen and dumped the contents on the floor. There were crystals, stones, pentacles, herbs, incense, candles and a book.

"I'm going to need a bowl of water and a knife if you don't mind," he said.

My jaw dropped. "You didn't come to apologize, did you?" I pointed accusingly at the collection of magical tools. "You *bluffed* me."

H shrugged. "I took a chance that once you came to your senses — thanks to my special chocolate — you would see that you're in danger and that I'm here to help."

I squinted at him and pursed my lips. He reacted by bowing his head and manifesting a purple rose, then held it up as an offering.

I took the rose and smelled it. "You're smooth, buddy."

I clicked my tongue and retrieved the water and knife he needed to create a spell that would undo the locking curse. Louis uniquely arranged his magical aids.

Magic is very personal, and I've never seen two spells cast the same.

Sometimes the differences were subtle. Other times, they were so contrasting that it was hard to recognize that the spells were designed for the same purpose.

There were familiar themes, like the elements — fire, earth, air, water, and ether, but the rest was personal taste along with trial and error.

Louis lit the incense and the candle and started his chant.

"Once these binds were coupled — They handicap the faithful — Disentangle these shackles — Break free from the connection — Turn on the enemy."

He took the knife and held it over the flame until it was intensely hot. Then he put the tip in the water and let it sizzle briefly. Gently, he touched the obsidian chest with the blade. It popped open like a jack-in-the-box.

"Beautifully executed," I praised.

Louis bowed exaggeratedly. "Why thank you, ma'am."

We both stood over the box and peered inside.

I reached out and hovered my hand over the items without touching them. "Something's off. I can't sense my magic." I backed my hand away.

Louis did the same thing but with both hands. "Nothing — there is no power here." He stopped for a moment, held his hands close to my crystal, and then whipped it away and slammed the box closed.

"What the *hell* Louis? What if we can't get it open again?" I said, confused.

"Good. Your instruments are cursed," he declared. "Not only that, I felt my magic being pulled from me. Just like before when you soaked up my magic."

I looked from him to the black chest and back to him. "Can we break it?"

I wasn't sure how hard it would be. "I don't have any experience with curses. My last coven, Golden Crescent, always practised *clean* magic. The covens High Priestess, my mother, taught us witches that dark magic was dirty and anyone using it would find themselves *soiled*."

"Golden Crescent — I know that coven. Your mom is Diane?" Louis asked.

"That's right. Do you know her?" I asked.

"We met briefly. There was a meeting between the High Priests and Priestesses of a few of the surrounding smaller covens when Shelley went missing. We were focused on finding Shelley and discovering Sacred Twilight's hidden motivations. I can see *now* the similarities between you and your mother. Her energy was graceful and kind — not that yours isn't — but you've been hiding, and Holly's been cloaking you from me." He scratched his head absentmindedly,

"You're full of surprises. So you were allowed at the meeting because Shelley's a member of your family?"

"Well, that too, yes. I was the one who called the meeting; I'm the High Priest of the Lunar Pyre," he answered.

Bruce jumped up on the couch carrying one of Louis's mojo bags and dropped it on my lap. I picked it up and felt the magic flow from the bag into my body.

Magic is alive, and it swirled inside me as if searching for something, then it seemed to dissolve like a drop in a puddle.

I handed the bag to Louis. "Check this."

He took the pouch from me and turned it over, scrutinizing it. "It's void of my magic." He looked at me with furrowed eyebrows. "What did you do?"

"Nothing, I just picked it up and instead of feeling the magic, I drank it up. I'm sorry, I can't control it," I explained.

"Don't be sorry. I'm just trying to understand what's happening. I have no previous experience with the dark arts, but I've been reading about them extensively over the past year."

"Do you know what's wrong with me?" I asked.

"I'm not entirely sure, but I suspect that Holly is some witch-succubus hybrid. The roomers of her sexual prowess are almost legendary." He rolled his eyes. "Holly's slept with half the city, and if she's drawing energy from several hooch hounds, none would feel the effects enough to realize what she's done. They'd feel flu-like symptoms afterward and probably assume they've caught a bug or something."

"And you know this how?" I asked, tilting my head.

He folded his arms. "It's not what you think. She doesn't get close to me, but people talk, and I've gathered information from dozens of them who *hooked up* with *her*. They all have the same pattern, cold and flu-like symptoms afterward. They don't make the connection, but I do."

Louis told me many of the Inn's staff members, who'd been with Holly, recounted their escapades.

Over a couple of hours, he explained in rich detail what the men and women Holly had lain with experienced. We couldn't find a pattern among the victims. It seemed she targeted anyone and everyone.

"I was advised that my dependence on magical instruments was a handicap and that once I put these *childish* things away — as Holly put it — my energy would be ten times more powerful." I leaned back on the couch and folded my legs underneath me.

"She said at first I'd experience withdrawals that would weaken me, but like the metamorphous from caterpillar to butterfly, it was a necessary stage in my development."

"She's a *parasite*," Louis spit.

I nodded. "Your chocolate was amazing, and the mojo helped me feel a little less foggy, but I'm nowhere near my usual self. How will I get my magic back?"

"You should perform the *Drawing down the Moon* ritual; it's almost midnight. The Goddess should be able to help with that," Louis said.

"Yeah, I usually do this alone and *naked*. I'd prefer if you waited in the kitchen or something." I tightened my lips and gave him a severe look. "It's a little early in our relationship for you to see me like that; *I'm not Holly*."

He laughed and put his hand up defensively. "Relax, I'm not a pervert. I'm here to help."

Louis went into the kitchen, and I dropped my cotton gown, stepped out of it, placed my feet apart, and raised my arms to welcome the Goddess. I felt a tangible sensation that the Goddess was making herself known as magical energy surrounded me.

I began to speak, "I am the vessel...."

Louis came flying back into the living room. "Stop," he shouted.

"Shut up, Louis, now I have to start over," I scolded.

He picked up my gown and covered me with it. "That's not the *Goddess* you're drawing down."

THE STAR

*L*ouis was right — I could feel it. Swiftly, I threw my loose-fitting gown over my head and started to tremble.

Louis began chanting something in a forgotten ancient language; it would have been distinctive to his coven. He picked up his wand, circled me, and zigzaggedly traced a sphere.

"I can't believe the power she wields. I've never heard of anyone blocking the Goddess like that before." I walked to my bedroom and added a sweater and some cozy socks to my outfit.

When I returned to the living room, Louis was squinting at my phone. I didn't hear the chime because I walked away. It must be Holly; no one else would message me this late.

"Why would she send that?" Louis asked.

"Can you sense anything from it?" I asked, ignoring his question.

"No, as I said before, Holly is a black hole when it comes to her and her coven. When I probed, it felt like I'd dropped a brick into a bottomless pit. I don't think she's blocking the Goddess; she's blocking you." He put his hand on his chin thoughtfully. "I saw her name and a tarot card on your display."

I picked up the phone to see that she'd sent a photo of *The Star* this time. The seventh card of the spread was supposed to represent my attitude and my effect on the environment. *The Star* also represented the promise of a brighter future.

"This is how Holly guides me through the *Magic Passage*," I said.

"Never heard of it. What's a Magic Passage?"

"It's the ritual that Sacred Twilight designed to initiate members into the Fourth Degree." I shrugged.

His eyes widened. "Fourth? That's unusual, of course; everything about that coven is abnormal."

I figured there was no sense in keeping the initiation a secret from Louis anymore. Without the full power of my magic, I couldn't battle against Holly's influence alone. I worried about how disappointed my mother would be if she found out I'd fallen into this trap.

"The Magic Passage is a metaphorical birth canal," I started to say but was interrupted when Louis began to laugh out loud.

"Naturally, *Holly* would use the *birth canal* as her initiation ritual. That nightmare of an ogress is so twisted." Louis shook his head.

I folded my arms. "Can I finish explaining?"

"Sorry, go on," he said, stifling his laughter.

"The symbolism was *supposed to be* about rebirth — not female genitalia," I emphasized sarcastically. "She evoked a spirit from another realm to manifest in our world and help her provide challenges for me using the Celtic spread as a roadmap."

Louis interrupted again. "She evoked a spirit for this?"

"Yes, that's what I said. Let me finish."

He rubbed the back of his neck. "Okay, sorry, I'm just trying to keep up."

"So this spirit she summoned was supposed to prompt her to

choose the card and affect the environment around me for spiritual enlightenment. Then we'd discuss the card, comparing it to the circumstances I was encountering, and she would judge my interpretation." I sighed deeply.

"That's it?"

"Pretty much. You were expecting more?" I asked.

"No, but I didn't want to interrupt you again."

"So?" I probed

Louis sat straight. "My first question is, how long is this supposed to last?"

"Around two to three days. This one is the seventh card, and it's after midnight, so I suspect the other three will come later today. Unless she realizes I'm on to her and cuts me off."

"Oh, she's not going to cut you off, of that you can be sure. She has some sinister motive and won't give up that easily. Holly's powerful, and I'd wager she's dedicated too," he said.

"Don't I know it."

"I can't believe you're involved with evocation. Didn't your mother teach you how dangerous that practice is?" Louis admonished.

"Please, Louis, don't lecture me right now. Let's focus on how to deal with this."

"We don't have much time. You could ignore her messages, block her number, and stay at my place. I can shield you until her influence wears off," he said.

"That would probably be for the best, except there's a blizzard. We should probably wait until morning." I yawned.

"Okay, I'll stay on the couch," he said, gathering up his enchanted items and placing them in his satchel.

"I'll grab you a blanket."

I went to the hall closet and brought a lovely fluffy quilt. I had two that could be alternated weekly when I did the laundry.

I handed him the folded blanket, and for a moment, our

fingers touched. I felt the sharp electric energy snap towards me as my body tried to steal his energy.

"Thanks," he said, pulling away.

"Sorry about that. I can't control it," I said.

"It's okay; your body's like a vacuum for magical energy right now — so depleted that it's created a vortex. Magic flows into you and off to some abyss instead of the natural energy exchange that usually occurs."

"I wonder how much magic I've lost. I feel heavy again," I said.

"Get some rest and leave your phone in the kitchen. I'm not sure how she's doing it, but Holly is milking your magic from you." He frowned.

"Okay, goodnight," I said.

"Goodnight."

I put my phone on silent and left it on the kitchen counter. Bruce followed me to bed and curled up near my feet. Laying there, I felt like my bones were aching. I tried to turn off the light using a simple spell, but nothing happened.

I resented being so gullible and vulnerable. I was afraid I'd never regain my magic. I got up, physically flipped the light switch off, crawled under my sheets, and closed my eyes.

"Sophia, *wake up.*"

I thought I heard a voice calling out from the darkness, and I strained to listen. I felt myself bouncing around annoyingly, and I couldn't understand why. Slowly I lifted my eyelids to see Louis was right up in my face with a wild look in his eyes.

I yawned and stretched. "Jeez, Louis, what's the matter?"

"Nothing's the matter with me. You were calling out in your sleep," he said.

Daylight shone through my bedroom window behind the curtain; I sat up and looked around. "What was I saying?"

"You were calling for your mom. I'll let you get dressed — we should go soon." He left my room.

I dressed in jeans and put on a heavy wool turtleneck. Usually, I wouldn't travel anywhere on a Sunday unless the Sandberg Inn called me for a scheduling emergency.

After washing my face and putting my hair in a French braid, I followed Bruce to the kitchen, where Louis was sitting with a business-like posture at my kitchenette.

He pointed at my phone. "She's been calling you all night."

"Who? My mother?" I yawned again and picked up my phone.

"No, Holly."

"I don't want to talk to her," I said.

"You should. We need to figure out a way to lead her off to determine our best course of action. I thought about it last night. She must have put Shelley through this *Magic Passage* of hers." He scowled.

"Perhaps," I said.

"Whatever happened wasn't good because we never heard from her again." He rubbed his head.

"Something went the way that Holly wanted it to," I suggested.

"What do you mean?" Louis asked.

"I didn't want to make you lose hope, but the vision I had of Shelley was in a flame that I lit — she was in anguish. I'm sorry, but I'm afraid she isn't with us. That's why you can't find her."

Louis went pale, and it looked like I'd kicked him in the nuts. He put his head in his hands and went silent. I wanted to put my hand on him to console him, but I would only end up stealing his magic.

"I already know. I didn't want to admit it to myself. As a High Priest, I failed my cousin. I should have prepared her better for the opportunistic monsters of the world. Evil craves power more than anything, and the magical realm is full of it," he said sadly.

"Do you still want me to call Holly and play along?"

"Absolutely not. You go ahead and call her and put her on video chat so that I can see her and — more importantly so that she can see me," he said firmly.

I scoffed. "Are you sure?"

"I am."

I selected video chat. She answered after the eighth ring.

"Well, Sophia, I see you've broken almost all the rules," she said scornfully.

"You can cut the crap, Holly. We know you've been using me." I snapped back.

She ignored my words. "Did you see the last tarot?"

Louis leaned closer to be in Holly's view, and I sat back. "Yes, we saw your fixed little magic card game. Drop the act — Sophia isn't participating in your filthy ritual."

Holly laughed delightedly and clapped her hands. "Oh Louis, you amuse me. I've noticed that you've been immune to my charms but don't fret; I have other ways to accomplish my goals. Now back away; I'm talking to Sophia."

"*Release me*, Holly."

"What do you mean, Dear?" She smiled cynically.

"I mean, let me go. Give me back my magic and stop syphoning it from me," I demanded.

"I can tell you didn't perform the *Drawing Down the Moon* ritual like you were supposed to. If you had, you would've had your magic back already — and then some. I'm not doing anything to you, the spirit is guiding me with the tarots, and *the entity* is the one that's interfering with your abilities." Her words were so smooth it was like she sang them.

"You're such a liar, Holly," Louis said. "The dark magic you've been projecting surrounded her and corrupted her attempt to summon the Goddess."

"Sophia, I don't know what happened — *I wasn't there* — but it seems you were, weren't you, Louis? Why don't you explain to Holly why you're interfering?"

"Shut up," he said.

"I will not. Sophia, it would be best if you search inside your-self. No one has taken your magic from you. The spirit has put Louis on your path to create a greater challenge for you to over-come. The dark magic is coming from *him*," she said.

"That doesn't make sense. Look at what I found when you were sleeping, Sophia." Louis walked to the living room, and I picked up my phone and followed.

He reached into his pocket and threw some herbs in the air. Bruce pounced on them and rolled on his back so that his orange fur was speckled with green and brown flecks.

Then Louis opened his arms wide, and a ball of blue energy appeared between his hands. It grew as he chanted — *reveal - detect* — three times until the blue electricity rose and settled like water collecting in the groves.

On my roof was a colossal pentagram overlayed with a bunch of ancient symbols that looked like they might be demonic. The signet absorbed Louis's blue energy and quickly turned invisible once again.

"He put that there last night, Sophia, while you were sleep-ing. Beware, he's dangerous." Holly cautioned.

"She's not a fool, Holly," Louis said.

"Listen, I'm no longer interested in the *Magic Passage*, so please call off your entity and leave me alone," I said.

"It doesn't work that way, sweetie. I told you in the begin-ning that when I evoke this spirit, I create a mission for it; until it accomplishes *that*, there's nothing I can do to stop it. I'm a medium, not a puppeteer. I can only offer guidance," she said.

"I don't believe you," I countered.

She ignored my words completely. "I'll offer more assistance to help you get through the final cards. *The Star*, Sophia, what does it mean to you right now."

"No," I said.

"It's your effect on the environment. You must see the calm

after the storm. The confusion will go away; stand firm against adversity. A brighter future is on its way for you. Keep going, Sophia." She blew me a kiss and hung up.

I blinked a couple of times, then looked at Louis. He was standing comically with his mouth agape.

"That arrogant she-devil," he growled.

She was trying to create doubt in my mind so I would be suspicious of Louis. It might have worked if she hadn't mentioned the word *puppeteer*.

Before, when I had enough power to summon an image, I saw the fingers with the yellow string tied to them.

I didn't recognize it at the time but now that she brought it up, and I think back, I remember that the fingers I saw were distinctly feminine.

"You've got to believe me, Sophia. Holly's a liar, and she's trying to manipulate you. I didn't do that." He pointed to the ceiling and stood still, looking at me.

"I know Louis, I believe you."

He let out a massive sigh of relief. "Thank the Goddess. I was worried for a minute there. At first, I couldn't believe she dared to accuse me. The *audacity* of that madwoman."

"She's a professional, that's for sure," I said disgustingly. "I need my powers back, and Holly must pay for what she's done."

"I want to know what happened to my cousin."

"Me too," I said.

"Let's gather some of your things and go to my place. Do you have a cat carrier? We should bring Bruce too." Louis pointed at the sleepy fuzzball lying on the folded blanket I brought for him.

It warmed my heart that he cared about my cat. "Yeah, I have one for vet appointments."

I gathered a small overnight bag, some toys, and cat food. Louis assured me he'd find a cardboard container that could be fashioned into a temporary litter box.

We didn't think I'd stay there for more than a day or two anyway. I packed light because we were concerned about how much of my stuff was cursed by Holly's dark magic.

The drive to Louis's townhouse was slippery as hell. He drove slowly because it was hard to see, and his car didn't have winter tires; I felt like we were skiing.

The radio announced that most major roads were closed because of the storm until the plows caught up.

We'd arrived at his place, and Louis's phone rang a moment after I let Bruce out of the carrier to explore.

"Hello?" He blanched. "I'm on my way."

"What's the matter?" I asked.

His face went ashen. "Katie's in the hospital. She's been in an accident."

QUEEN OF SWORDS

I didn't hesitate. "Let's go."

Katie was Louis's only sibling, and he was visibly upset. I put my winter coat back on and handed him his. He took it from me, threw it over his arm, and walked toward his stairway.

"I'll be right back; I need to grab a couple of things," he said.

While he went upstairs, I entered his kitchen and filled the cat dishes with water and Kitty Nibbles, Bruce's favourite food brand.

I took note of how tidy his place was. As far as I knew, he wasn't expecting any company — he was a neat freak.

He returned down the stairs carrying a fair-sized leather case, and behind him, a trail of mystical light flowed through the hallway.

"I'm putting up an extra barrier. Some of my protection spells have been probed — *I can feel it*," he said.

I took in a deep breath and let out a long sigh. "I'm so sorry if I've gotten you into something that puts you and Katie in danger."

"You?" He opened the front door and motioned me to go

outside into the snow squall. "You didn't get me into anything. I've been involved since Shelley vanished."

"I'm sorry anyway. I'm not used to being so helpless," I said.

"I need to take care of my sister first, then I'm going to fix you up," he promised.

The way he spoke made me believe him. It was so odd to see Louis like this. He was always such an easy-going nerdy guy.

He wasn't a herculean man, but now that I saw Louis — the High Priest — handle his magic and take charge, I was impressed.

"Tell me what happened; who called?" I asked.

"My mother." He leaned over the steering wheel to better view the snow-covered road. "She said the hospital called. Katie and two of her friends were driving through town for breakfast — of all the *stupid* things to be doing during a blizzard."

"Did she say anything about what kind of condition Katie was in?" I asked tentatively.

Louis's jaw clamped shut, and it looked like he was grinding his teeth. He turned the steering wheel left onto a road I couldn't see because the white flurries were so dense.

He was using his magic to drive, and I ought to let him concentrate. We went a little further down the road and turned right.

It was scary; I couldn't see what he saw. I tried to use my mind and reach for clarity, but I sensed nothing.

"My Mom said the driver's dead, and Katie and the other girl are in critical condition." Louis swallowed hard.

We drove the rest of the way to the hospital in silence. He parked near the entrance, and we ran into the emergency department —straight to the nurse's station.

"I'm here to see my sister Katie Nelson. She was in a car accident; she would have just been admitted." He shifted his weight swaying back and forth.

"She's been moved to a room; please have a seat, and

someone will be with you shortly," the nurse said.

Louis sprinkled some light powder on the counter. "That's wonderful, but I need to see her now. What's the room number, Nurse Kendall?"

Clever, Louis was hypnotizing the nurse to give him the information he wanted. She huffed a frustrated sigh, looked down at the clipboard, and then over to her computer screen.

"If you *need* to see her, the doctor has moved Katie from intensive care to room three-fifty-three for observation." She turned her chair away from us and started typing on the keyboard as if we weren't there.

Louis strode off, and I followed him, almost jogging to keep up. When we got to Katie's room, he threw open the door without knocking. "Katie?"

"*Louis*," she exclaimed.

I stepped into the room and closed the door behind me. Katie had her arms wrapped tightly around her brother's neck.

She was sniffling and trying to hold back the waterworks. The tears had been flowing steadily from the looks of her puffy eyes.

"I'm so glad you're okay," Louis said.

She looked over at me and back at Louis, and I could see that she was communicating something unspoken to her brother.

"You can speak openly in front of Sophia; she's a witch too." He told her.

"Oh Louis, it's awful. Mike died, and Fiona's hurt." She hugged herself as her eyes darted around the room as she remembered the tragic event.

"The weather's terrible, Katie. Why were you guys out in it?" Louis said softly; it wasn't time to give her trouble.

"Oh, Fiona and Mike wanted to try out the new restaurant, and he drives a big four-wheel sport utility vehicle. We were going slow until the other truck came after us."

"What do you mean?" Louis asked, and he looked at me

suddenly.

"A big black truck came behind us and bumped the back of Mike's truck. It was scary. I used a spell to ward the truck off, but it didn't work." Her eyes were wide with shock.

"Someone ran you off the road?" I asked.

"Yes." She let out a light sob. "Who would do something like that? I don't understand why my magic couldn't stop it. I used a protection spell when I couldn't ward the truck off. It all happened so fast — I couldn't save Mike, and Fiona is in *bad* shape."

"How about you?" Louis said, gently walking around the bed and inspecting her for damage.

"I was banged up pretty good, but I've been overdosing on healing spells using the technique you taught me." She put her fingers on her temples. "When the truck started to flip in the air, I panicked, tightened my protection spell, and sheathed myself in my magic. I should have widened it to protect Mike and Fiona. I'm so sorry, Louis; I was so afraid." She started crying.

Louis sat on the bed with his arm around her, and I passed her the box of tissues from the bedside table.

"It's not your fault Katie, and I know you did your best. I'm so sorry to hear about Mike. I will go see what I can do for Fiona." He stood up and looked at me. "Sophia, will you stay with Katie while I check on her friend?"

"Yes, of course, I will." I nodded and sat on the bed; Katie reached for my hand.

"Ouch, what was that?" Katie's eyes opened in surprise.

"Sorry, I forgot," I winced, thinking about the shock she must have felt after using so much of her magic.

It takes energy to protect and heal, and my body tried to steal the power she had left.

"Yeah, until we figure out how to fix her problem, it's best not to touch Sophia — she's been cursed," Louis said.

Louis slipped out the door, and Katie looked at me, puzzled.

"Who cursed you?" She blew her nose.

Just then, my phone chimed, and I knew it was another card. I pulled my phone out of my pocket and held it up to see what Holly had sent this time. It was the *Queen of Swords*.

"Oh, *that* hussy," Katie said, peeking at the name displayed.

"I guess you know her," I said.

"Oh yeah, that cow seduced my cousin Shelley into her creepy cult. She's threatening you with that tarot card?" Katie asked.

I felt my face flush red from shame. "I guess she is, yes."

Katie must have noticed because she grimaced. "She got you too, eh?"

"She did." I nodded. "She convinced me to give up all my magical tools, and in my weakened state, she somehow managed to poison me. Now I can't seem to access my powers. Whenever I encounter magical items or people, I absorb the energy like a black hole." I shook my head. "The worst is that it doesn't fill or replenish me when I take it in. I get a little boost, and then it's gone."

"Sounds like you need a new alternator," Katie suggested.

"Alternator?"

"Yeah, my loser ex-boyfriend was a mechanic. If your alternator fails, you'll have a dead battery, trouble starting, and slow malfunctioning accessories. Sound familiar?"

"Okay, you lost me," I said.

"I don't know *exactly* what I'm saying; my special ability is linkage. Louis teases me and says my superhero name is *Katie the Connector*." She scoffed.

Louis came back into the room and closed the door behind him.

"How is she?" Katie asked

"She'll be okay; I was able to knit her bones together to speed up the healing process. I stopped the brain bleed, so she may have mild concussion symptoms, but she'll be spared a coma." He rubbed the back of his neck. "There is nothing I can do about the misery she's going to experience when she wakes up and finds out that Mike passed away."

"I'll be there for her." Katie looked at me. "Louis is a healer, Sophia; that's the hardest magic to perform," she said proudly. "By the way, big bro, that harlot Holly sends Sophia pictures of tarot cards to threaten her." She shifted to lay back on the bed, moaning slightly from the pain.

"Already? Which card this time?" he asked.

"*Queen of Swords*," I said. "This will be the eighth card she's utilized to manipulate my circumstances. In this case, the card points to the atmosphere and influences around me."

"That's a threat," Katie said. "In a negative aspect, that card is a liar, cheater, and disloyal. All attributes that describe *Holly*."

"Katie and Shelley were close," Louis said as if to explain Katie's extreme distaste for Holly.

"My cousin was my bestie," Katie said, brushing her fingers through her short bangs.

"Katie thinks my alternator is broken," I said to Louis.

"Does she? That's interesting. Every witch has a unique attribute to their magic. Katie makes connections between seemingly unrelated objects. She's always on the mark so far as I've experienced."

"I experience visions, well I used to anyway," I said.

"No mystery why Holly targeted you. I wonder if she gains your abilities when she snatches your magic?" Katie remarked.

"That's an interesting question," I said.

"We should let you get some rest," Louis said.

"Don't you dare leave; I don't want to be alone. For all you know, maybe Holly put the hit on my friends and me." She shivered at the thought.

Louis sat on the bed with his sister, and I sat in the sterile plastic chair. "If I had my magic, I could use my clairvoyant visions to answer these questions."

"Can you heal her, Louis?" Katie asked.

"Well, I don't quite know where a person's alternator is." Louis flipped his palms and looked at me. "Nor how to cut Holly's connection to you if she's feeding off your energy."

"Let's get out of here and search through your Book of Shadows." Katie swung her legs to the side of the bed.

Louis stood up and put his hands on his hips. "You're staying here."

"No, the hell I'm not, *Louis*. Where are my clothes? Sophia, can you find me something to wear?" Katie asked.

I didn't want to get between brother and sister here, and I kept my mouth shut. I sat in the chair, staring at the tarot card Holly sent while the siblings had it out with each other.

Katie won the dispute when she promised to defy Louis and call a cab as soon as he left. She sassed that going with her brother — a highly talented healer — was the safest option. I had to give it to her; she made a good argument.

"I'll get you something to wear; just wait here." Louis groaned.

Soon after he left to confiscate some clothes for Katie, Holly called me. I looked at Katie and put my index finger to my lips to silence her, and she nodded understanding.

I walked to the corner of the room with my back against the wall and answered. "Hello."

"Sophia, where are you?" Holly asked.

"At the hospital, Louis's younger sister was in a car accident." I watched her face for any indication that she had something to do with it.

I was appalled when she laughed. "The *Queen of Swords*, Sophia?"

"*Screw off*, you malignant tumour." I hung up.

"Oh my *God*, is she for real?" Katie gasped.

"I'm so pissed off that my hands are shaking," I said.

"She's going to pay for this. We need to understand what

she's done to you." Katie stood up and grabbed her purse. "It's better that we get out of here before she strikes again. We're unprotected here."

Louis returned soon after with someone's clothes; they weren't Katie's, that's for sure. They were a few sizes too big and belonged to an older person from the style.

Katie didn't complain; she dressed quickly and followed us out of the building. Louis explained that he cast several confusion spells and signed Katie out.

Katie and I stayed quiet while Louis navigated his way through the storm and back to his place so that he could concentrate. The last thing we needed was to end up in a ditch again.

When we went inside the warm interior of his townhouse, I heard Katie let out a little squeal.

"Who are you? My goodness, you're a pretty kitty. Yes, you are."

"That's Bruce," I said, smiling at her as she scooped him up off the floor and carried him to the kitchen.

"I didn't want you to lose focus by upsetting you until we got out of the hospital and through the storm, but Holly called again," I said to Louis.

"Oh yeah — Sophia told her right off. Can you believe that pig laughed when Sophia told her I was in a car accident? She probably had one of her dunce boyfriends run us off the road and kill Mike," Katie fumed from behind the fridge door.

She pulled out some cream and poured a couple of teaspoons into a bowl. "Just a little bit won't hurt him."

"No, and you've made a friend for life," I said.

"Say something, bro. What are we going to do?" Katie looked at Louis, who hadn't responded yet.

He glanced at Katie and then back at me. "I'm not sure, but Sacred Twilight is *going down*."

JUSTICE

*K*atie opened the fridge, grabbed a jug of tomato juice, and poured us a glass. "Drink up; it's got Louis's mojo in it."

"Thank you," I said.

"I'm going to have to sit; I still feel woozy. Healing magic helps with wounds, but it takes a lot out of you." Katie made herself comfortable on the couch.

"I'll be down in a minute; we'll need my Book of Shadows — I also want to check a few of my older occult books. We'll start by attempting to restore your access to magic," Louis said.

Sitting with Katie in the living room, I felt a profound sense of comfort in the spiritual hothouse surrounded by magic.

Louis must have carefully crafted a magical haven against invasive energy. I was already feeling a little more like myself.

Katie picked up a laptop from the coffee table and opened it. Louis came back downstairs with his arms full of old books and scrolls.

"There should be something in here that will help us." He put the literature on the table and separated them into two piles.

"This is all the information I have on dark magic." He pointed to an enormous pile on the left. "And this is everything else."

Katie wrinkled her nose in disgust. "I'll stick with the internet."

Louis and I sat on the floor. "I'll take the pile of dark magic; if any of these have been enchanted, I can't do any damage." I waved my hand toward the giant pile. "You take that heap."

"Sure, you just want me to do all the heavy lifting," he smirked.

I smiled back at him. "Well, you've read through it before, so it should be easier for you."

"Since I have most of the grimoires, I'll look for a way to reestablish your connection to the mystical realm and heal you so that you stop seeping magic," Louis said.

"Why don't you call it the quantum realm? I mean, that's what it is." Katie flipped her hand and produced a beautiful apparition of an atom with a shiny pink nucleus and three blue electrons swirling around it.

"Beautiful," I said.

Louis held his hands out, and a green and yellow dragonfly appeared with sparks of light cascading off its wings.

"Because it sounds too scientific, at least when we use the word magic, it brings spiritual images to mind. Science fails to describe the *majestic* life force of the universe," he said.

Katie looked at me. "He's so *flowery*."

I tilted my head sideways and smiled.

We all dove into reading, and after a couple of hours of failure, I found something interesting that might help us.

"Have either of you ever heard of a wraith?" I asked.

Louis squinted, and Katie shook her head, so I elaborated. "It's a legendary creature that feeds off the souls of other beings. What if Holly is some variation of a wraith but feeds off of magic instead of spirits."

"Let me see that, Sophia." Louis dropped the papers he was holding and held out his hand.

I passed it to him and watched his facial expression as he read the description in the ancient scroll.

"I found something, too," Katie said. "Young adults have been disappearing from Sandberg every winter."

"Really?" I asked.

"This caught my eye because fifteen years ago, the police department released a statement about a young man who disappeared without a trace. They found pentagrams in his apartment and assumed he ran into some foul play with some Satan worshippers." She huffed. "I hate the stigma; if you practise any sort of witchcraft — people assume you worship Satan."

"People have been disappearing in the winter for fifteen years?" I gasped.

"More than *that*," she emphasized. "I used my intuition to search the internet for a correlation."

"Could you search Magic Passage?" I asked.

"Magic Passage, sure. Is it some incantation?" Katie clicked away at her keyboard.

I snorted. "That was what Holly called the initiation into the Fourth Degree in her coven. The Magic Passage symbolized rebirth."

Katie opened her mouth and gagged. "That *gross wench* — leave it to Holly to create a *ritual* around her *genitals*."

"Your brother said pretty much the same thing," I said.

"I think you're both on to something." Louis interrupted. "We need to act fast; you're in greater danger than I thought. This wraith creature is in a few more passages here and over here."

Louis pointed to a couple of time-ridden scrolls that were so old they crackled when he opened them. Katie and I moved closer to see.

In all the records of encounters with the beast, the victim died after having their souls consumed.

"I don't understand; in these accounts, the records describe wraiths that feed off people's spirits. But it's my magic that's disappearing," I said, puzzled.

"That's just it, Sophia; it's not your magic that she's stealing — she's consuming your life force. Your spirit is stronger because you're a witch. You can't use your powers because all your energy is being diverted to keep you alive. If we don't stop her soon, you'll die." Louis's voice trembled.

My phone chimed — *Holly*. I looked at my phone to see the picture of *Justice*.

"Which card?" Louis asked.

"*Justice*, the ninth card," I said.

"We need to hurry; Holly is using the tarot cards as a countdown. She's guiding whatever demonic spiritual entity she's evoked with cards. Leading you off just enough so she can stay latched to you without raising suspicion," Louis declared.

I felt weaker; Louis's magic wasn't staying inside me. "I need magic to build energy and replenish my life force, but Holly is devouring it soon after. It's a deadfall either way." I scrolled through my contacts. "I need to call my mom."

Louis reached for the other pile. "I've found a grimoire that described a spell to engineer magic that quickly dissipates. We should be able to provide you with magic orbs that will pop like a bubble. It won't last long, but at least you'll feel the positive effects, and it will dissolve before the wraith can leech the energy – buy us more time."

"What's the matter, Sophia?" My mother answered, sounding alarmed.

I put her on speaker and placed the phone on the table. "Mom, I'm in trouble," I said.

My mother listened intently while I explained to her that not only was the coven I joined run by a wraith, but I'd fallen into her trap and was in danger of losing my life.

Louis and Katie added a few details about the *Sacred Twilight's* reputation. Louis reminded my mother that they'd met at the council concerning Shelley's disappearance, and Katie read a few articles from the internet that brought her up to speed with the history.

"A coven of serial killers," Katie stated with anger and disgust.

"The roads are closed; even if I wasted my magic on clearing a path to you, I fear it would be a waste." My mom sighed. "Louis, I believe your plan will work; I'm going to contact my covenmates and have them all send power to you. You'll be able to create more of that fleeting magic at an accelerated pace. Sophia, use the brief flashes of power to liberate yourself from Holly's dominion. Be aware she's not going to give up easily."

"I understand," I said.

She was in full High Priestess mode. I knew my mother would be terrified for my welfare, but she was wise enough to see that fear wouldn't help. Strength and experience were what could save me.

"Katie, you help Louis deal with the force of magic coming in his direction. Louis, prepare yourself for the *intensity of this energy*. I'll contact my coven, and we'll begin right away," my mother said.

Louis cleared his throat. "I'll be ready."

"Me too," Katie added.

"Sophia, I love you. We're going to end this today." She hung up.

Seconds later, my phone started to ring. "Speak of the devil."

"Don't answer it," Louis said abruptly.

We let it ring, and Louis scurried around his townhouse, gathering an athame, some crystals, candles, incense, a wand, and a compass. Katie prepared the altar and fashioned a cauldron. When I didn't answer, Holly sent a text. I picked up my phone to read what she said.

"Holly sent a message," I announced.

Katie groaned. "What does it say?"

I read out loud. "*Sophia, there's no turning back from the Magic Passage. It leads one way. Because you've broken your pledge to Sacred Twilight, I have no choice but to enact Justice for your transgressions against the coven.*"

"It's fine. Let her spew her *nonsense*. We have work to do." Louis made no effort to hide the contempt in his voice.

I felt nauseous from the effects of my life force being drained into some unknown mystical void. Louis recited some ancient language and constructed a packet of refined energy approximately the size of a bowling ball.

The spheres swirled with purple electricity. Bruce popped his head out from behind the couch to watch the orb rise in the air like a soap bubble. It crackled and sparked, and the four of us stared at it while it hovered.

Louis finished his incantation and looked at me. "You ready?"

I yawned and felt weaker than before — whatever Holly was doing to me didn't physically hurt but made me sleepy. "I am."

"I'm going to let it go. You're like a vortex for power. It's going to race into you, and you'll have a few seconds before it dissipates. While you temporarily have your powers, you must search for the source of the parasitic entity that's consuming you."

I yawned again and had trouble keeping my eyes open. "I'm feeling sleepy. Let's start."

I imagined that carbon monoxide poisoning was similar to what I was experiencing — tasteless, odourless toxin.

Louis unclenched his hand, and the purple electrical ball flew at me at lightning speed. It hit me like ice water. I expected it to be warm.

I felt energized, and something alien squirmed inside me. The magic was like crisp winter air that rushed into a boiler room — I felt refreshed. The feeling waned quickly, and I saw that Louis had fashioned another electric ball.

"I can feel your mother and the Golden Crescent magic flowing into me. I'm not sure how they've managed to give me this boost, but it's working. Here comes another." Louis said, opening his hand.

Another blast of glacial energy smacked me. I loved it.

"Try to use your ability, Sophia," Katie reminded.

I was so engrossed in the rejuvenating feeling that I'd forgotten to summon visions. I attempted to focus on Holly, but the power disappeared. I looked at Louis, and he slammed me with another ball.

This time I took advantage of it. I pinched my eyes shut and reached out to find her. I could smell her skanky perfume and hear chanting, but the magic faded too rapidly.

"I'm going to send it faster, and it's going to dissolve quicker. The magnified magic is making it easier." Louis flipped his hand.

Another ball came at me, and they kept coming faster. I moved my mind closer to Holly by starting where I left off before the previous vision faded.

After a few more strikes, I could see her through a dense cloud. She was standing in the centre of a room surrounded by her coven mates. The vision faded.

"She is using the full power of her coven; they're all in on it," I cried out.

Louis was focusing hard, and I could see he was having trouble controlling his energy. Katie saw it, too, sat closer to him, reached out and held his hand.

It was getting breezy in the room from the electricity. I needed to turn things around before filling that ghoul with my magic.

I swayed backward when another bolt hit me. "I need the athame."

Katie handed me the enchanted dagger. Handling spellbound objects would feed Holly, but I had a hunch.

I swiftly took the handgrip in one hand, placed the other over the butt, lifted it in the air, and brought it down full tilt into my thigh. I screamed, and as the energy ball hit me, I saw Holly in my mind get swept off her feet.

Shocked by my scream and concerned for my welfare, Louis stopped creating the magic and rushed to inspect my leg. He attempted to grab the knife.

"No, leave it there," I hollered at him.

"What the hell are you thinking?" Katie said.

"I know what I'm doing, *trust* me." I looked into Louis's eyes; he nodded, returned to the cauldron and continued creating the exotic magic orbs.

"Louis can heal you," Katie said.

"Not yet," I said, grinding my teeth. "I need to remove the spirit. I've severed the connection temporarily, but they'll reestablish it soon. There's something dark inside of me, and I need to remove it."

Without being able to use salt or draw banishing symbols, I had to use my mental fortitude to fight off the entity that Holly was using as a tracker. I could feel it writhing inside me now, reaching with its tentacles to reinstate its connection with her.

Katie cringed at the wound. "Hurry, Sophia, you're bleeding out."

Louise's eyes flickered toward my leg and back to fashioning the orbs. He kept feeding them to me, and I used them to corner the beast inside me. I focused on forcing it toward my knee.

As soon as another frigid orb hit me, I concentrated on chasing it down my leg, then I took the knife's hilt and twisted it. I could hear the creature scream as it ripped itself from me.

"Sophia," Louis cried out.

He rushed to me, placed his hands over the knife, and used his magic to pull it out of my leg and seal the flesh behind it. After a few waves of his hands, I only felt a pinching sensation like I had a charley horse.

"Wow, I can't believe how fast you can heal," I exclaimed.

"Thanks to your mother, my talents are souped up right now. How are you feeling?" he asked.

"She doesn't have her claws in me anymore, and the spirit she evoked is gone." I breathed a long sigh of relief.

"Oh, no." Katie sniffed.

"What is it?" I looked at her as she picked up Bruce.

Katie wiped a tear from her eye. "She killed your cat."

THE HANGED MAN

My phone chirped, and I could see that the final tenth card on the display banner revealed *The Hanged Man*.

"Get away from me, you bitch." I threw my phone across the room, livid.

"Louis, *do something*," Katie demanded.

Louis hustled to Katie, gently took Bruce from her, and put him in the cauldron. I was frozen still, overcome with grief.

Louis started chanting — *arouse* — repeatedly while blowing smoke into the vat. He sprinkled some flower petals inside and started to stroke Bruce.

I snapped out of my stupor and lightly rubbed Bruce's chin. Katie joined in, and Bruce began to stretch, yawning. I wiped my eyes and wet cheeks — I didn't realize I was crying.

"That was the power of love," Katie whispered as she caressed the kitty, who started purring, pleased with all his attention.

I let out a sigh of relief, picked him up, and nuzzled his fur. "Don't scare me like that, baby; thank goodness you have eight more lives."

I called my mom and put her on speaker.

She answered right away. "Sophia, give us good news. I'm on a conference video call with the rest of Golden Crescent."

I sniffed. "We're all good here. Louis had to resurrect Bruce, though."

I told her about *The Hanged Man*, the tenth card indicating the outcome of this Magic Passage. We supposed that Holly sacrificed my cat since they couldn't get to me because of my allies.

We could hear through the phone that my mother rang a small bell to ward off evil. "The wraiths are vicious creatures; I'm grateful Louis and Katie are with you. We'll continue to focus magic but directly on you this time Sophia."

"Okay," I said.

"Hopefully, it will enable you to restore access to your abilities — plus give you a little extra. Use your telepathic vision to locate Holly. *Any* evidence you come across may be useful. She wasn't working alone."

"Holly's time has come; I'm ready," I assured.

"And Sophia — I'm glad you're okay." She said softly before hanging up.

"I bet your mom is a force to be reckoned with," Katie said. "I can't believe she didn't panic."

She looked at Louis. "Our mom would be a basket case if Louis or I were in your shoes. He's the composed one in our family. That's why he became the High Priest of Lunar Pyre after our grandmother died."

Katie returned to the laptop to search for any other information she could dig up online. I rummaged through Louis's objects to collect a few items I needed to help me centre and then zone in on the villains.

He went into the kitchen to prepare a potion to speed up my healing from the damage I'd suffered. We didn't know what harm the parasitic entity that had inhabited me for the last few days might have done.

"Do you have any vinegar?" I asked.

"Yes." Louis came from the kitchen and handed me a bottle.

I took it from him and poured a few drops into his fragrance oil burner, along with sage and frankincense. "Thanks; I have a homemade spell to assist with clairvoyance."

"Whatever you need," he said.

I lit the tea-light candle with the snap of my fingers. It was remarkable how amazing it felt to have the use of my supernatural abilities again.

The vinegar odour wasn't very pleasant, but it would help me differentiate between magical illusions and true oracular visions.

I held an amethyst in each hand and reached into the mystical realm for Holly and the rest of her Sacred Twilight disciples.

It didn't take long for me to get results. With augmented magic, I saw dozens of telepathic visions from Holly and her minions' past, present, and future. There were so many that I wasn't quite sure of the timeline, but I could generalize the events that led up to my experience with the cult.

I tried to focus on Holly in the present; her coven was scrambling around with gasoline; it looked like they were preparing to burn the building they were in.

I was abruptly cut off as she turned and looked in my direction. She squinted her eyes momentarily; then her eyebrows rose in shock. She waved her hand in the air, and I lost the connection.

"I'm pretty sure she saw me," I said.

I put the crystals down. Holly used powerful sorcery to protect the covenstead activities with extra safeguards after sensing my presence.

Louis returned from the kitchen and handed me a cup of brown liquid that looked like coffee but smelled like ass.

I recoiled. "What *is* that?"

Louis pushed it toward me. "Plug your nose and drink it down at once. Don't think — drink."

"Oh, you're so poetic, Louis," Katie mocked.

I did as I was told and slugged it back. The only thing worse than the smell was the aftertaste. My stomach gurgled, and I thought for a second that I would hurl.

"Did you perceive anything?" Louis asked.

"I sure did. Time affects clairvoyance by making the visions further away in time fuzzier. I gathered as many visions of events as possible. Then I pinpointed the vivid images to locate the coven's current whereabouts," I explained.

Katie closed the laptop and put it on the table. "Don't keep us in suspense; what did you see? Do you know what happened to our cousin?"

I cringed. "Yes."

Katie saw the expression on my face and clenched her jaw.

"Tell us," Louis prodded.

"They burned her on a pyre. Holly — or the thing pretending to be Holly — is an evil, wicked monster. When Shelley tried to escape and return to Lunar Pyre, Holly decided the *pyre* would be a fitting way to torture Shelley," I said, folding my hands on my lap.

Louis's lips tightened into a thin line, and Katie wept.

"Continue," he said flatly.

"I reached back as far as possible and discovered that none of Sacred Twilight are witches. They're all unearthly wraiths who've been hiding in the shadows for centuries. They fed on people's spirits until they came across a witch. Then they developed an appetite for the supernatural power it gave them."

"They sound like demons," Katie snuffled.

"I didn't get that impression. They seemed more sinister — if you can believe it."

"How so?" Louis asked.

"They could wield magic themselves after a few lunar cycles of suckling the witch life forces. The difference was that they couldn't enchant objects or charm talismans and amulets," I said.

I scratched my head. "I saw them try, but I'm going to venture a guess that because the energy is stolen, they're incapable of creating magic; they can only use it."

"How old is Holly, or whomever she is?" Katie asked.

"I don't know, but she's been around for hundreds of years. I saw only two of them far back in time, but it was blurry. She recruited other creatures and consumed the underlings if they couldn't successfully feed on witches. Her taste for the power of magic is so great that she's not satisfied by regular people."

Louis started to pace around the room anxiously. "Did you find anything that will help us hunt them down?"

"I think so," I said. "I sensed their hive mind, a telepathic connection between them. We should be able to use it to our advantage. Subdue the leader and the followers will weaken and disperse."

Katie reached for the laptop and opened it. "I found something interesting as well. Right after Shelley disappeared — look at this video. Watch when I play it in slow motion."

Katie played last year's broadcast from the local station. There was a crowd of people standing behind a barricade that was put up by the police and fire department. The reporter was talking about how the authorities suspected arson was the cause of the fire.

"You think that's where they murdered Shelley?" Louis asked.

I squinted at the spectators for a moment and then saw it. My face must have changed because Katie started to nod.

"You see her, don't you?" she asked.

"Where?" Louis hunched forward to get a better look.

I pointed at a woman standing in the crowd behind the reporter. "Right there."

It was Holly, but her face kept flickering.

"She can mesmerize people, but the camera reveals her true nature. Katie, can you slow it down?" Louis asked.

She looked at me and pursed her lips. "I'm the techie in the family."

Katie zoomed in on Holly's image and tapped the arrow to control the video speed. Slowly she inched it forward in time.

We watched as Holly's face metamorphosed into what could only be described as a spider.

"*Damn*, she's *ugly*." Katie paused the video. "They're bugs?"

"Something like that," Louis said.

"Figures," she said.

"They're killing witches to live longer and hide their true identity," I said disgustedly.

Katie scowled. "I thought spiders lived in solitude."

"Some live in aggregates," Louis remarked. "There is even a variety that exhibits swarm behaviour."

I picked up my phone and opened my search engine. "The question is, how do you trap a spider?"

"It seems that these wraiths don't like enchanted objects, and it's common knowledge that spiders hate strong scents," Louis said.

"That's probably why they forbid you from using your supernatural goodies," Katie said.

Louis nodded. "And, you might've caught on that they couldn't use instruments, only redirect magic from themselves. Enchantment of physical objects requires inherent magic — as you said before, I suspect wraiths are incapable."

I stood up and stretched. My leg felt good; Louis's magic was amazing. I walked over to the window to find it wasn't snowing anymore.

Louis phoned a couple of covenmates from Lunar Pyre and asked them to do some research.

Katie informed me that Lunar Pyre consisted of young witches. Their grandmother and other members of the original group had passed away, leaving a small coven of seven.

I redialed my mother. "Hey, mom, we were able to uncover some information."

"What did you learn?" she asked.

"Sacred Twilight is an aggregate of spider-like wraiths that feed off witches to become powerful and live longer. Holly is their queen, and they've been getting away with it for centuries."

"Bloody parasites," she sneered. "I will consult my Book of Shadows to see if I can dig up something that may help us. Tell me, how did these peculiar creatures spellbind you, Sophia?"

"I don't know, Mom; I'm pretty ashamed of it. I barely survived after being captivated and practically hypnotized into falling for their queen's trap — the *Magic Passage*." I said meekly.

"Magic Passage?"

"Yeah, that's what Holly called the initiation ritual that would give me fourth-degree status in their coven. She convinced me that I would be more powerful without magical aids and have the ability to evoke and control spirits in the physical world."

"Sophia," she exclaimed. "I taught you that's dangerous."

"I know, *believe me*, I regret it, Mom. Holly's rebirth ritual was her way of fattening me up for the kill."

"Don't be too hard on yourself. From what you've told me, these are deadly organisms that have been perfecting their snare for much longer than you've been alive. You managed to escape."

"I didn't do it alone," I pointed out.

"No one does, Dear," she said. "I have an idea."

Her first suggestion was to get everyone involved from both covens. Some were familiar with each other from a year ago when they convened over Shelley's disappearance.

Once, we had everyone on a conference call, Louis, a High Priest and my mother, Diane, a High Priestess, took turns explaining the situation and describing the enemy we were up against.

The witches randomly made suggestions and offered improvements to each other's ideas. Eventually, we collectively came to a short list of weapons we thought would be effective against the enemy.

"The consensus is that a hodgepodge of every witch's most powerful and favourite talismans and spells will be gathered and prepared for a mass assault. Now we need bait and a location; any proposals, Diane?" Louis asked.

My mother responded. "The bait is going to have to be Sophia. As far as these creatures know, they're only contending with you, Sophia and Katie. Without the entity that inhabited Sophia, they won't be able to perceive the rest of us backing you up."

"How will we trap her?" I asked.

A few recommendations came through from various witches until Katie spoke up. "I say we meet her at what's left of the old abandoned building they burned my cousin in."

No one spoke at first. Then one at a time, support came in for Katie's proposal. It was unanimous.

I wasn't fond of being referred to as bait. I preferred to think of myself as a tantalizing trap and looked forward to obliterating Holly and Sacred Twilight.

"How are we going to *lure* them?" Katie asked.

"That's a good question. Sophia, you're the one who spent the last year hanging around Holly while she groomed you for their ceremony. What do you think is a good way to draw her to the site?' Louis asked.

"If I detected a weakness in Holly, it would be her arrogance. I can recall several instances when we would be out somewhere, and she'd get annoyed when she didn't have all the attention and the upper hand," I said.

"How will that help us?" a witch from Golden Crescent asked.

"She hates being ignored or treated commonly and covets the spotlight — probably because she had to hide in the shadows for many years."

"You want to ignore her?" Katie asked.

"No, I want to *taunt* her."

"How?" my mother asked.

I searched through Louis's collection of witch supplies. "Louis, do you have a tarot deck?"

"No, sorry."

Katie jumped up. "I do." She ran upstairs and returned with her backpack and a deck of Egyptian tarot cards.

"What's your plan?" Louis asked.

"I'm going to change the rules of her silly game and provoke her."

THE EMPEROR

"*H*ow do you plan on doing that?" my mom asked.

"I'm going to text Holly a card this time." I flipped through Katie's deck until I found the card I was looking for — *The Emperor*.

"Any particular reason for that card?" Louis asked.

"I think we can all agree that Holly never prepared a Celtic Spread. She selected the cards ahead of time to manipulate me."

Witches murmured in agreement, and Katie wrinkled her nose in disgust.

My mother gently shushed the group. "So why do you think that particular card will trigger emotions in Holly?"

"I was thinking about my clairvoyant visions of her when I looked backward in time." I stared at the picture of *The Emperor* in my hands.

"The further back I went, the fewer wraiths were in the group. It was a little foggy, but my oldest vision was of Holly and a single male figure. It looked like he was reprimanding her for something. I could see him standing over her while she knelt in front of him."

A witch from Louis's coven spoke. "Why not send her the High Priest card?"

A couple of people agreed, and I listened to them come up with a reason for using the card that could be interpreted to represent the male leader of a coven. I listened carefully but remained convinced *The Emperor* would be the best choice.

"They are wraiths, not witches. I don't think they respect our hierarchy at all. They are just using our magic and our traditions to their advantage. Holly sensed me probing her, cut me off at the end, and put a wall up. She knows my abilities. She would know that with her guard down temporarily — I dug into her background."

"I see where you're going with this," Louis said.

"Holly has elevated herself over her current group, but in the past, she either feared or adored that guy she bowed down to. Strong feelings like that don't disappear," I said.

"Yes," my mother said. "I see now. *The Emperor* represents a leader or father figure, getting what he wants through force. An empiricist."

"Right, there will be no mistaking who the card is portraying. Holly's done her research over the years regarding tarot cards. I think she'll crack and come for me when she sees it." I tented my fingers and waited for the witches to discuss my proposal.

All the witches agreed, and everyone was coming for the battle. We had to figure out how long we needed to prepare the trap.

Now that their magic didn't need to be focused on amping up Louis or me, the witches could use their magic to open the snowy roads and clear a path with a few spells.

Each one gave a precise estimated arrival time with extra added to gather talismans and enchant additional items. We took the longest time from the furthest witch and added one hour to set up.

"*The Emperor* card, a picture of the abandoned building, and three hours typed on the bottom. That should do it, agreed?" I asked

They all agreed, and Katie put together a collage with the two pictures and a clock showing three o'clock, the time we decided.

She sent it to my phone. We informed the group of witches that we were ready.

"You three go in the front door," Mom said to Katie, Louis and me. "Holly and her gang of wraiths will see that you brought your two friends — she'll be expecting that. We'll park at the adjacent building, enter through the back entrance, and attack at once."

"Good plan, Diane," Louis said.

"See you all soon. Let's get off the line and get going so Sophia can send the message before these wraiths split and run. Be careful." Mom hung up.

I looked at Louis and Katie, who were already gathering anything imbued with magic or looked decent to enchant. "I'm sending the text now."

The three of us remained still while we waited for a response. If there were none, we would continue with the plan and hope she'd show up.

After a couple of minutes, my phone chimed in response. Katie jumped and flew to my side at breakneck speed. Louis was already close enough to see. I opened the phone, and we all saw the *Ace of Disks*.

I put the phone back in my pocket. "She's coming."

We had extra time to prepare because we were the closest. If Holly decided she and her minions were going to go there early, it would just mean they would have to wait in a half-burned abandoned building.

We were going to show up fifteen minutes before three and prepare to set the trap.

We spent the next couple of hours putting extra magical energy into as many enchanted and bewitched items as possible. Time flew by, and we collected everything in a duffle bag and piled it into Louis's car.

The main roads were already plowed, but the snow was pretty deep on the side road in the industrial area. I recited a spell we'd learned from Golden Crescent during our conference call to clear the snow from the road.

I was relieved to see how super effective it was, knowing that the streets would not hinder the arrival of our backup.

We got there first. There were no tire trails in the parking lot when Louis pulled in.

"Perfect, they aren't early," he said.

"Let's get set up," Katie opened the door and jumped out before Louis turned the engine off.

She opened the trunk, grabbed the duffle bag, and marched toward the entrance on a mission. Louis and I followed behind her.

She recited a quick spell to unhinge the padlock on the door and pulled it open with her free hand.

"Look at that," Katie gasped.

The corner of the open warehouse had scorch marks that led up the wall. Behind that were sheets of plywood that boarded up the area that had been thoroughly damaged by the fire last year.

Louis walked toward the stain, blessed it with a spell for the dead, and sprinkled something where his cousin died.

Katie and I emptied the duffle bag, took all the items, and created a four-foot-wide circle with contents. Louis spray-painted sigil traps around the walls and on the floor.

We heard a couple of cars pull up. I wiped the dirty window to see six vehicles had pulled in and parked in a semi-circle around Louis's car. Katie joined me and swore under her breath.

"Don't worry," I told her, figuring she was scared at the entourage that showed up.

"Oh, I'm not worried. You see that black truck there?" She pointed.

"Yes, that's Jamie's," I said.

"Look at the bumper."

I saw what she meant; there was a huge dent. "That's the truck that ran you off the road?"

"Yes, that *savage* killed my friend Mike," she growled.

Time was up. I could feel the presence of the other witches; I wasn't the only one with telepathic abilities.

One of the witches from Louis's coven used my eyes to see what was going on from their standpoint. This way, we wouldn't have to signal — they'd know when to enter.

We noted that all twelve wraiths from Sacred Twilight showed up in the parking lot.

Katie and I rushed back to where we had created the circle and motioned Louis to join us.

We were inside the magical protection circle when Holly and her accomplices entered the building. It consisted of lit candles, citrus incense, an assortment of crystals, various talismans and ceremonial daggers.

Holly wrinkled her nose and curled her lip in disgust when she saw us surrounded by magical weapons. I held a dagger, Katie a wand, and Louis had a wooden staff with a beautiful transparent red garnet at the top.

Holly laughed. "Look at the three of you — so cute. Your little power circle is no match for us."

"Bastard, you rammed my friend's truck; you aren't getting away with that," Katie said, glaring at Jamie.

"I see you found Shelley," Holly chirped, pointing at the black stain on the floor behind us.

Katie made a move to lunge. "You…"

Louis grabbed her arm to keep her in the circle, and Katie shut her mouth.

"Don't let her get to you," he said. "She's just trying to goad you so that you break the circle."

"Don't worry, I'm not falling for it," Katie said.

They were pretty good actors, I thought to myself. The circle was part of the ruse; we needed them in the building with their guard down so the rest of our collaborators could surround them.

As long as they were focused on us, they shouldn't try to escape before we could spring the trap.

Louis drew their attention by pointing at the wall behind them, and a couple turned to see what he was looking at.

"They've got magic seals written all over the walls," Jamie said cautiously.

"No matter, Zeulcor. That might slow us down, but it won't stop us from leaving. It's time to feast," Holly said, and her face changed to its spider-like form.

Zeulcor must be Jamie's wraith name, I thought absentmindedly. Holly's subordinates slowly morphed to match her alien appearance.

They walked around the magic circle where the three of us stood and settled like a pack of wolves, ready to pounce.

Louis's clever drawings of the symbols on the wall tricked them into thinking *that* was our trap. They didn't suspect twenty witches were closing in on them.

I felt the witch watching the scene through my eyes exit my mind, and I knew they were on their way.

"We'll cross their protection barrier simultaneously; it won't be strong enough to stop all of us combined," the thing that used to be Holly sneered. "On my count of three, two...."

Suddenly the front and back doors flew open, and the windows smashed as twenty witches came *screaming* into the building.

I glanced at Louis; his eyebrows were raised at the powerful sound of so many howling witches.

All were dressed abundantly in amulets and magic scarves, each carrying their chosen magical weapons. The formidable collection of sorcerers was a fantastic sight.

They moved at lightning speed and circled the wraiths. Holly let out a screech that made my skin crawl, and the ghouls made a run for it.

Louis's magical symbols on the walls started to glow, and the witches fired magical bolts at the beasts. Katie and a member of Lunar Pyre moved in on Zeulcor, who had climbed up the wall like a demon.

My mom, Louis, and I focused on the thing that was Holly. She would flip and lurch at us one at a time, then squeal when we'd blasted her with magical energy.

One by one, the other wraiths shrivelled up into black fist-sized lumps of black stone and dropped to the floor. The witches could gang up on the remaining savages who were more robust.

Holly seemed to get stronger every time we took out one of her wraiths. It looked like just before the others perished, some of their energy shot into her, and she took on their power.

Eventually, all other wraiths were gone, and only Holly remained. We surrounded her. It took every witch present to manifest an incredible energy bubble that enclosed her.

Slowly it shrank until it made contact with her body. She scratched and shrieked ungodly noises that vibrated in my bones. Even a dozen banshees couldn't pierce my ears with their screams the way she did.

Finally, the beast that called herself Holly shrivelled into a chunk of shiny metal that dropped, making a dent in the floor.

"Gather them up but don't touch them," Louis commanded. "Diane, where will we put them?"

"I'll take them to consecrated ground, create a binding spell and bury them," my mother answered.

The clumps were gathered using levitation and magical tongs and placed in a sacred bag. None of us wanted to take any chances.

Holly's essence, or whatever her remains were called, proved so heavy and dense that it took five witches to lift it into the enchanted sac and tie it off with a powerful spell.

After we cleaned up the mess and removed the spells from the walls and floor, we gathered together to take stock of injuries so Louis could heal them.

My mother had a large gouge in her shoulder from Holly's talons. A few other witches suffered minor injuries and lined up to receive Louis's exceptional healing magic.

I went to each witch to personally thank them for saving my life and showing up to rid the world of the hideous creature that tormented our kind.

I spent extra time with my mother; she hugged me tight and made dinner plans for the following weekend. She insisted I bring Louis and Katie as well.

"I'm going to go home and reassure my husband that our daughter is fine and give him the good news that we have claimed a victory today," my mother said.

After everyone departed and we were in Louis's car driving away, Kate asked. "I take it your dad isn't a witch?"

"No, Dad isn't gifted. My brother and I inherited the magic gene from Mom."

"Louis and I inherited it through our grandmother," she said.

We drove Katie back to the hospital to spend time with her injured best friend. She also wanted to express her condolences to Mike's family, who'd been leaving her messages.

Louis convinced me to stay at his place since Bruce was already there. The offer of my favourite meal — spaghetti — easily persuaded me.

* * *

WHILE LOUIS PREPARED THE MEAL, I sat on his living room floor with Bruce curled up on my lap, reading Lunar Pyre's Book of Shadows. I was fascinated with how similar it was to my mother's book from Golden Crescent.

"A lot of the spells, charms, and enchantments in this book are familiar," I remarked.

"It should be; our covens originated from a common source hundreds of years ago," Louis informed.

"Wow, I didn't know that."

"My grandmother passed down some scrolls that described a healthy number of witches who were so powerful and numerous that they split into six different covens," he said.

"I wonder what happened?"

"Suppers ready," he said.

"Finally," I said. "I thought you planned to continue torturing me with that divine smell."

"It's just parmesan." He winked.

We ate dinner and enjoyed red wine. After cleaning up, we sat together, cuddled on the couch, watching television.

Bruce came trotting into the living room carrying one of the scrolls by the twine it was tied with. It was a ridiculous sight, and we both started to laugh.

"Let me have that before you wreck it, Bruce," I said.

He dropped it in favour of a chin scratch, and I picked up the scroll. I could feel the ancient power radiating off it and couldn't resist understanding more about it.

I held it in both hands, closed my eyes, and used my clairvoyance to reach into the past. I saw many witches dancing, celebrating, and living peacefully.

Then I sensed dark magic and saw shadow figures attacking the witches. The vision was fading, but I could hear a High Priestess whisper from the past — *The demon created the wraiths to hunt us; we must disperse.* I dropped the scroll like a hot potato.

"What did you see?" Louis asked.

"I saw something evil and heard a reference to a demon," I said, alarmed.

"I suspect we should do a little more research and investigate the magical history in this area. But in the meantime, come here." He put his hand around my waist, pulled me closer, and kissed me.

THE END

ACKNOWLEDGMENTS

Words cannot express my appreciation for all the family and friends, who have supported me during this writing adventure.

Alexander and Jana have given me the courage to put myself out there as an Author, and I'm exceptionally grateful for them.

Thank you.
   XO

COMING SOON

Dark Reaction - 2023

ABOUT THE AUTHOR

Jody Swannell is an emerging author of Contemporary, Horror, and Science Fiction.